Deadly Treats

Deadly Treats

Halloween Tales of Mystery,
Magic, and Mayhem

edited by Anne Frasier

NODIN PRESS

978-1-935666-18-9

Cover Lettering: Robin Ludwig Cover Design
Layout: John Toren

Library of Congress Cataloging-in-Publication Data

Deadly treats : Halloween tales of mystery, magic, and mayhem / edited by Anne Frasier.
p. cm.
ISBN 978-1-935666-18-9
1. Halloween--Fiction. 2. Horror tales, American. 3. Ghost stories, American. I. Frasier, Anne.
PS648.H22D43 2011
813'.087308--dc23

                                    2011022655

Nodin Press
530 North 3rd Street,
Suite 120
Minneapolis, MN
55401

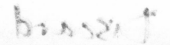

*to bag-toting kids of all ages, and to those who
work hard to make their holiday scarily special*

Contents

The Angel Deeb

Patricia Abbott

"Mr. Deeb?" A middle-aged Asian woman stood in the doorway, looking around. She'd no reason to know who I was in the midst of the crowded room, but spotted me immediately. I was the only white man in a threadbare clinic in the depths of Detroit. I rose, following her into one of the cubicles. "What brings you to see the doctor today?" she asked, motioning to the examining table. I looked at it warily; things were getting too real. Me, sitting on that paper sheeting, hearing the telltale crinkle beneath my sweating thighs. Imagine.

I cleared my throat, debating whether to tell her the truth. The facts were so ridiculous that I decided to be vague. "I'm having some problems with my back." I was mumbling and she leaned in to hear me.

"Lower?" she asked, jotting something on her clipboard.

I pointed to the spot. Both spots to be precise.

She looked at me over the top of her glasses. "When you say problems, do you mean you're experiencing pain? Do you have difficulty in raising your arms, for instance?"

We looked each other in the eye. "A bit." There was some tenderness but that was the least of it.

She waited for me to continue, but when I didn't, said, "Would you please take off your shirt, Mr. Deeb?" She handed me a gown, took my temperature, checked my blood pressure and pulse. "The doctor will be with you in a minute." The door closed behind her, and after hopping off that table, I began to read the cautionary literature covering the walls. Thirty-five minutes later, an Indian doctor, roughly half my size and weight, entered the cubicle. "Mr. Deeb," he said, holding out a delicate hand. I shook it.

He promptly washed his hands, glanced at the clipboard and said, "Back pain, huh?"

I swallowed. "Probably see it all the time. Right?" I was badly in need of some reassurance after the reading I'd just done. It was hard to believe anyone got out of here without a grim diagnosis.

"Back pain's a common complaint. Can you tell me more about your particular problem?"

I don't know why I was so reluctant to tell him. Was it fear of what he might tell me, or embarrassment at my...problem's... oddity? For several weeks I'd noticed a growth on both sides of my upper back. Felt it more than saw it, of course, because it was in one of those places hard to spot—even in a mirror. "I seem to have some sort of...enlargement." The word *growth* seemed laden with implications I didn't want to introduce into our conversation.

"See." I flexed my shoulders and the 'enlargements' appeared.

The doctor's face grew pensive as he began to examine me. After a minute or two, he straightened. "It's called a winged scapula. Or, in your case, scapulas. Your shoulder blades are pushing out. Have you always had them? Can be congenital."

"Noticed it for the first time a few weeks back." I'd turned over in bed one night and rocked on one of the little nubs. Twisting left, I quickly found the other one. I was a virtual rocking chair.

"Hurt yourself on the job recently?"

I shook my head.

"Play sports?"

No.

The doctor sat down on his wheeled stool, planting his heels on the floor to steady himself. "Well, you must have done *something*. Your thoracic nerves are damaged. Someone slam you into a wall?" I shrugged and he sighed. "What do you do for a living, Mr. Deeb?"

That was a question I didn't want to answer—maybe the real reason I'd put off coming here. Telling a doctor you're a pickpocket doesn't earn his respect. I'd never been asked about my occupation by a doctor before, but I had my share of queries from other sources and well remembered the looks I'd received in response. I was a thief, a petty criminal, a small-time crook. None of these professions garnered admiration.

"I'm unemployed at the moment." Not so unusual in Detroit. "I used to load trucks," I added, inspired. I loaded trucks for a paper company in the nineties. It was the best, if not the only, legitimate job I ever had.

The doctor smiled, pleased to have an explanation to hang my winged scapulas on. "If you heaved weighty merchandise, you may have done some damage. Odd that it didn't develop before now, but still…I'll give you some literature on your condition along with a set of strengthening exercises. Let's give it three months to see if things have improved. Of course, call the office if the condition deteriorates." He had me push against a wall, flex various muscles, raise my arms. He took several photos, even pulling a video camera out of a filing cabinet. "First time I've seen wings on both scapulas," he muttered, mostly to himself. The nurse showed me out, giving me several leaflets describing exercises to do. I made another appointment, paid my bill and left.

I read the literature thoroughly and began the recommended exercises. Thinking back on it, my natural ambidexterity was probably why it was a two-sided condition. And I decided it was reaching rather than throwing or lifting that had brought about the condition. I'd *reached* a lot over the last ten years: primarily into pockets or for purses dangling from shoulders or hands. Reached my hands across aisles and through windows on cars, buses, subways, trains. Lots of times—well, most of the time—the object I was reaching for was on the move: a man or woman walking down the street, occasionally someone on a bike. Once or twice, a car took off before I could take away my hand. Grabbing a purse, for instance, was rife with problems if it didn't easily detach. My long arms, which had served me well, turned out to be weakly ligatured.

I decided to stop reaching for things as much as possible, but I only had so many ways to make a living. I contented myself with mailboxes, the kind people install by the road. Problem was, often some nutcase would swing around the corner just as I stuck my hand into one—or the front door would open despite the bogus mail carrier's uniform I wore. I began to wonder if I was losing my touch. My hearing wasn't good enough now to pick up a car's motor before it closed in on me. My intuition also seemed to be faltering. I was the beneficiary of a declining skill-set in every way at thirty-eight years of age.

Despite doing the exercises, regardless of getting more rest and modifying my behavior, the wings continued to grow. Alarmingly. It became difficult to lie on my back, so I slept on my side with a pillow between my knees to ease the pressure. I needed to go back to the clinic and demand a specialist, but I didn't. It was just too damned weird. I'd built my life on being as invisible as possible, on fitting in without a fuss, and now I didn't. My shirts began to look odd, so I purchased larger jackets with shoulder padding to hide my growths. Soon I moved on to capes. More than once, I thought of the Kafka story I had read in tenth grade. Was I turning into something else? Was a meta-morphosis taking place?

After a half-dozen wasted efforts (empty mailboxes, ones filled with flyers or magazines), I finally stumbled on a box on a quiet suburban street. Red, gold and orange leaves drifted over the macadam as I studied my quarry from behind an evergreen. The size of the mailbox attracted me. The residents must be receiving packages of some heft to install this behemoth contraption. A scarecrow stood propped beside it, its arm draped around it. A plastic black cat nestled nearby.

Halloween was a holiday that meant little to me as a childless man, and its decorations even less. Creeping up, I pushed the stuffed doll aside, but luck wasn't with me. I heard the front door opening before I'd even fully pulled the mail out. Fleeing, I took the entire contents along—sticking it under by arm. Back to the car and departure post-haste. Had the occupant of 5 Pillsbury Road seen me? I was pretty non-descript except for the bulge under my cape. Back home, I sorted through the sizable packet of mail. What I was hoping for, of course, were checks I could quickly cash or financial information I could make use of. There were rarely any saleable items in mailboxes. No stray pieces of pricey jewelry or expensive electronics. Constant references to mail theft by the press had seen to that.

Today, there was a good-sized package from a medical facility, however, and although I generally kept my distance from drugs because of the people they attract, I opened it. Selling drugs might tide me over—painkillers, anti-depressants, Ritalin, anti-anxiety drugs. There was a market for almost any drug, and I knew a guy or two who would middleman it.

It was drugs, but the wrong kind. Along with the medication, the Styrofoam box was filled with Polar packs and air bags. The accompanying pamphlet contained instructions for administering insulin to a child. I'd intercepted a shipment that would soon expire if I didn't return it. A child was waiting for this at that house at 5 Pillsbury Road. It would have to be returned. None of my activity had ever endangered a child and I was not about to go down that path now.

I parked several streets away that night, not sure if my car had been spotted in the afternoon by whoever opened that front door on Pillsbury Road. It was a good night for loitering, being Halloween, and the late October darkness arrived quickly. I made my way along the suburban streets, just another costumed reveler among hundreds. Hadn't E.T. gotten away with this stunt thirty years ago? I'd left my cape at home despite the chill temperatures; my wings were freed for once. A hint of euphoria came with it, too.

"Look, an angel," a small boy cried, pointing. But I'd disappeared before his father could turn and question the height and weight of that angel.

My goal was to set the box on the porch, ring the bell, and disappear. It anyone spotted me I'd be just another costumed trick-or-treater. I made my way to 5 Pillsbury Road. The front walk was plagued with skulls and tombstones, and I nearly put my foot inside an overturned squash.

"You're here then," a tiny but assertive voice said from the bay window nearest the door. The child was about six, I'd guess, and dressed like a princess. A gold crown perched lopsided on her head. Her hair was too short and messy to pull off the headpiece though.

"Me?" I said, looking around. "I think you have the wrong guy." I placed my package on the step and turned to go.

"Then you aren't my guardian angel?" She adjusted her crown, using her reflection in the window for a mirror. A line of winking pumpkins on a table outside lit her view.

"No, I'm just trick-or-treating. Same as the rest of 'em." I motioned to the distant hordes and began to skulk down the walk.

"Not me," she reminded me. "I'm stuck inside." She paused. "And that's sort of ridiculous, you know. A grown man trick-or-treating." She peered at me through the dark. "Those aren't real wings then?"

"Nope." I was nearly at the gate and turned. "Hey, see that package on the porch?" I pointed. "It's for you." I pointed again when she didn't move. "You might want to fetch it and take it inside." Where were her parents? "It needs to go in the fridge."

"I can only open the door if you're my guardian angel." She was quite adamant. "I'm not allowed to open it to strangers."

I sighed. Maybe I *could* be her guardian angel for the length of time it took her to open the door. "Okay, I'm your guardian angel."

"I thought so. And those *are* real wings?"

I nodded and fluttered them, rising a few inches at the same time, something I hadn't even known I could do. I heard a deep intake of breath, and then she smiled and disappeared, opening the front door a few seconds later.

"You shouldn't open the door to strangers," I said as she picked up the package. "This is the one exception. You need to get that package into the refrigerator pronto."

"I know what it is," she said, sounding bored. "It comes every week. I was hoping you'd bring me a greeting gift."

"A greeting gift?"

"You bring one to your hostess when you come to their house the first time. Something like guest towels, flowers, or coasters made of tile." She frowned. "Or in my case, perhaps something more suitable for a princess."

"Never heard of that custom before. Look, why don't you shut the door now and I'll be on my way. You're going to catch a cold."

She returned to her position at the window before I could escape. "What's your name anyway?"

"Deeb," I said, without thinking.

"That's a funny name for a guardian angel. I suppose I can get used to it though."

"Sure, call me Deeb." What did it matter if we never met again?

"You can call me Princess Isabella." I nodded. "And next time you come, try and remember to bring me a greeting gift."

I nodded again. "I'd better be off."

"I especially like barrettes if you can't think of something." I was at the gate now and held up a hand. She waved back. "See ya," she yelled.

The streets were filled with children. Taking a circuitous route in case I was being followed, I made my way back to the car. There was a tattered wallet on the road beside it. It had fifty bucks inside and nothing else. I pocketed the money surreptitiously. Well, even angels have to make a living, I told myself. And one good deed a day was enough.

At least until I grew into my wings.

Sunlight Nocturne

Bill Cameron

Early on the morning of October thirty-first, three intruders entered a home on the east side of Lents Park in southeast Portland. The date sticks with me because it's the day I'll finally get around to building the bat house I've been talking about for the better part of the year. I catch the breaking story on the morning news while I drink my coffee and scrape cobwebs from my eyes.

Word is, one invader kicked through the front door and bludgeoned one of the occupants—identified as a nineteen-year-old Mormon boy from Provo named Jeremias McCreevey—as he slept on the couch. Dead at the scene. The other occupant, a seventeen-year-old pregnant girl, tried to flee through the back door, only to meet the other two attackers. They shot her in the belly, then tore through the house spilling drawers, slitting open upholstery, and ripping into the sheetrock walls with a claw hammer until they were interrupted by approaching sirens. The girl had managed to drag herself into the backyard and dial 9-1-1 on her cell phone before losing consciousness.

McCreevey's mother, haggard but anxious to talk, told a Provo television reporter she thought her son had been sharing an apartment in Gresham with two other LDS boys. She had no idea who the pregnant girl was, nor why her boy had to die. The girl—identity withheld pending notification of next-of-kin—is being prepped for surgery at Emanuel Hospital as *KGW Sunrise* gives way to the *Today Show*.

For all that, I'm more interested in the weather report. The day will be dry and unseasonably warm, the last gasp of an extended Indian summer which has been lingering since mid-September. I drink another cuppa joe to Matt Lauer's nattering and feel grateful for being a year-and-a-half past the time when I might have gotten the call-out on the deadly home invasion. It's one of those days when it's good to be an ex-cop. Not Detective Kadash, just ol' Skin.

I spend half an hour rooting through my garage for the screwdriver, staple gun, and a quart of grey house paint I vaguely recall buying a year before. No sign of the paint. I take the tools and bat house kit onto the front porch for what I expect to be a long day of low-level bloodletting and streaming expletives fit to make a Teamster blush.

When I emerge, the sun is peeking over the shoulder of Mount Tabor and tinting the front lawn bronze. It's still cool, but the feather touch of sunlight hints at the day's warmth to come. I smell dew on the air as I start sorting the pieces of the kit on the porch. It's a simple three-chamber roost with interior baffles pre-roughened so the bats will have something to grip. I'm just starting to make sense of it all when I hear the tap of tiny footsteps on my walk.

I look up to see little Danny Bronstein approach from across the street, trailing his mother behind him.

"I'm sorry, Skin." Luellen blows her bangs out of her eyes. "He saw you outside and wanted to come over."

"Danny's always welcome. You know that."

She smiles gratefully. "Did you see the news this morning? That boy and his girlfriend?"

"Yeah. Unfortunate situation."

"They haven't caught the guys yet. Someone called in a tip and the police tracked them to a house down around Foster and

82nd, but they went running off in different directions. Cops are everywhere now."

As if to punctuate her report, I hear a *whap-whap-whap* in the distance. Off to the south I can see the hovering chopper. It's too far away to tell if it's a news or police helicopter, but the location is consistent with activity on the ground in the vicinity of Foster and the mid-80s.

"Bad guys on foot?"

"I'm not sure."

"I'll be right back." I go inside and turn on the radio, tune to OPB. They're on the national report at the bottom of the hour, so I increase the volume enough to hear on the porch and rejoin Luellen and Danny.

"Might as well keep up with what's going on."

Luellen's eyes get distant for a moment, but then she focuses on the pieces of wood on the porch. "What's this stuff?"

"It's a roost. For bats."

"A roost for bats."

"That's right. The inestimable order Chiroptera, which around here is represented mostly by the little brown bat. I'm going to hang it on the front of the house over the flower bed."

She's quiet for a moment. From inside the house, I hear a reprise of the weather report. Blue skies and heat. Danny fidgets on the lawn. "It's almost winter. Are bats still around?"

"I know. I'm late." No need to mention I bought the kit in February with bold plans for a spring installation. "If nothing else, it will be ready for next year."

"Oh."

"You sound worried."

"It's not that. It's just …"

"Weird."

"Well, you're a weird fellow."

I chuckle. "And yet you still live across the street from me."

"Actually I was wondering if you could watch Danny for a little while. I've got to pick up some things. I can take him with me, but you know how it is."

"Of course. He can help me paint the roost."

"If you want smudges and handprints, he's your man."

"That's exactly what I want."

Danny sits down on the stoop next to me, fascinated by the pieces of wood and screen which make up the kit. Luellen kisses his forehead with a wet smack, and laughs when he rubs the spot dry. "Thanks, Skin. I'll be back in an hour or so."

"No worries."

Danny is a quiet boy, as well-behaved a four-year-old as I've ever encountered. Give him something to do and he'll be content for hours. I let him hold the screws. He watches my every move. From the living room, I hear an update on the home invaders. One has been picked up after rear-ending a UPS truck on Foster as he fled toward Powell in a stolen Ford Focus. The others remain at large, presumed armed and dangerous. The girl is still in surgery.

"What are we makin', Mister Skin?"

"It's a bat house."

He ponders that bit of information. Passes me screws when I ask for them. I manage to get the whole thing together without drawing blood from either one of us. Together we regard the assembled house. Two-and-a-half feet tall and eighteen inches wide. Access from the bottom. My plan is to mount it under the eave, south facing. Decent sunlight even in the dreary months.

"Do bats live in houses?"

There's a note of concern in Danny's voice. I can't tell if he's worried about the bats which might come to live in this house in particular, or about houses in general.

"Not in your house."

He screws his mouth up into a skeptical little knot.

"Bats eat bugs, you know."

He eyes me sideways. Then he runs his hand over the smooth outer surface of the bat house. "What kind of bugs?"

"Mosquitoes and stuff."

"I don't like noskeetoes."

"Me either. But the bats will eat them for us."

"Okay."

His mother appears shortly after that and scoops him up. "Sorry, Skin. The morning got away from me."

"We didn't even notice. How long were you gone?"

"Too long. The police are still chasing those guys. They have them cornered in a house over near 50th and Division. I was stuck in traffic for half an hour."

She's anxious, her expression a mirror image of Danny's when he contemplated the natural history of the Chiropterids. Luellen likes things quiet and safe. Citywide manhunts fall outside her comfort zone. She thanks me and then hustles Danny across the street.

I put my tools away, drift inside. Turn off the radio. The helicopters are still flying. The sound of their rotors beats out a cadence which carries me back to my tour of Vietnam. I remember lying wrapped in my poncho at sunset and watching fruit bats fluttering through the jungle canopy, the motion of their membranous wings ethereal and hypnotic.

Long time ago.

I drop onto the couch, hit the power button on the remote. Russ and Brenda, the KGW morning news anchors, are back for the noon report. Two suspects remain at large, but police are questioning the fellow who crashed into the UPS truck. I know how that will go. The cops probably already know who the other invaders are. The bastard will make sure the first story on the books is one that paints him in the best light. "I thought we were visiting a friend. They never told me it was no break in until the door's busting down." I've had the conversation myself dozens of times, variants thereof. These guys are always badasses until you get them in the little room and give them the stink eye.

They show Sky 8 video from the crash scene, then the dead boy's mother is back, still baffled about what he was doing in that house. His fellow missionaries from the apartment in Gresham claim they haven't seen him in months and thought he'd returned to Provo. It's a pretty good guess whose baby it is, but Mother McCreevey doesn't want to discuss that possibility. The girl is still in surgery; the baby was delivered via C-section and is now being treated in the neonatal intensive care unit. A boy.

When the news ends, I step out onto the porch. A warm, dry breeze carries the smell of illegal leaf burning, a comforting scent. The midday sun hangs low and watery in the southern sky as a reminder of the winter bearing down on us. I hear the fearsome bickering of sparrows and the first juncos of the season, then the skir of skateboards. A pair of skaters wheel down my street and for a moment I stare at them. I've known a few in my day, one in particular, but it's been a long time since I've seen him. Damn memories again. I wait until the skaters pass, then head across the street. I've given up on the can of paint.

I knock on Luellen's back door. Through an open window above, I can hear her singing quietly to herself, a song I've heard many times before, a tuneful lullaby. At my knock, the singing stops, and a moment later she opens the door.

"Oh, Skin. Hi."

"Hey. I thought Danny might want to come watch me hang the bat house."

"I don't want to be any trouble."

"It's no trouble. He seems interested."

"He always likes visiting with you. After his nap okay?"

"Great."

While I wait, I pull out the ladder and make sure the battery for the drill is charged. The helicopters move nearer, then farther away. I'm not really keeping track, but it's hard to not wonder where the action will move to next.

The big break in the case comes before Danny awakes. The skell in custody ID's McCreevey's mother from a frame grab off the TV news. Police confirm she flew to Portland the week before, a round-trip which carried her home again the same night. They figure that's when she hired the crew. The idea was to scare her wayward boy, trash his house, get him to turn away from the new life he'd chosen. She didn't count on Jeremias being armed, less on the fact he couldn't shoot for shit. When the bullets started flying, one of the invaders bashed his head in with a stone paperweight from the coffee table. The girl had already been hit.

Northwest Cable News shows tape of Mother McCreevey being taken into custody by the Provo police. They have to censor part of what she's shouting as they put her in the back of a patrol car, but I hear enough. "I wasn't going to lose my boy to no bleep-bleep city trash." I turn off the TV and head back outside.

Luellen and Danny join me. I climb atop of the ladder, balancing precariously on the step warning me NOT A STEP, trying to wield the drill without screwing my hand to the lap siding. I manage to center the roost between two windows and get it reasonably straight. My neighbors will complain when the guano starts to streak the siding, assuming a bat ever moves in. Whatever. It's not like I don't own a hose.

Luellen takes the drill from me as I descend the ladder.

"What are you passing out tonight, Skin?"

"I usually pass out in front of the TV trying to find a channel that isn't showing *Law and Order* reruns."

"Not when. What?"

I stare at her.

"You don't have candy, do you?"

"Why would I have candy?"

"It's Halloween, you big ninny."

"Ah." October thirty-first. Right. "I've been distracted."

One of the attackers is still loose, but the main hunt is tapering off. The police know the only gun involved was McCreevey's—recovered at the scene—so they're focusing on known associates, friends, relatives of the remaining fugitive.

"You've got to have Halloween candy. I'll pick some up for you."

"I could just sit on my porch with a Super Soaker."

She ignores that. "Why don't you come trick-or-treating with us?"

Danny gazes up at me, expectant. I smile. "Sure. Why not?" I sit down next to him on the stoop. "What are you dressing up as?"

He thinks for a moment. "It's scary."

"The scariest thing I can think of is a starling."

Danny giggles. He knows how I feel about starlings.

"Scarier."

"A zombie starling?"

Luellen rolls her eyes. "Skin, you're hopeless." But she's smiling as Danny tumbles on the porch, his giggles too much for him. Luellen holds out her hand. "Come on, sweetie. Let's go get you ready."

It's some time after four when Luellen brings little Danny back across the street. He's wearing a black fleece skullcap which she's cut so a point dips across his forehead to the ridge between his eyes. His outfit is black as well, an inside-out sweatshirt and black pants. A black cloak drapes across his shoulders and hangs almost to the ground.

Luellen crouches next to him and smiles up at me.

"Show Mister Skin your costume, honey."

His eyes are wide as he lifts his arms. Luellen has trimmed the cloth cape into the shape of bat wings. He gazes at me, face solemn.

"I eat bugs."

I nod. "Important work."

He shows me his teeth for a second to emphasize the point.

"But not too many at once, I hope. You need to save room for candy."

At that, Luellen smacks her forehead. "I forgot his candy

bucket. It's in his room." She smiles quickly and a little sheepishly.

"No rush. We'll wait."

Danny looks up at me. "It's a pumpkin with lighted eyes."

"Sounds like a good one."

"It is."

While we wait, he throws up his arms and runs around my lawn, flapping his wings and squeaking. I watch, smiling, and imagine him snapping up insects in flight. I'm sure his mother would be aghast but the thought gives me a chuckle. Danny frowns my way, disapproving of my laughter at his important work, and squeaks more loudly. In the dry grass, his footfalls sound like the rustling of crepe paper.

But the smile dies on my face when a guy rushes out of my back yard through the side gate. There's no easy way to get back there except through the house or the way he came. But from the scratches on his face and exposed forearms, I assume he arrived the hard way, through my neighbor's raspberries and over the cedar fence at the back of my lot. He's got a Skeletor thinness to him, his neck long and ridged, his Adam's apple an angular prominence. His arms are veiny and laced with tats, muddy blue prison work. In one hand he's holding a shaped block of red granite. I can't decide which of us is more surprised. His mouth falls open to reveal a nasty case of meth mouth. Danny stops near me and points.

"Too many bugs."

His voice is no louder than a dove's coo, but the fellow hears him and raises his inked arms in alarm. At a glance, the tats look like poorly rendered spiders and flies which seem to move, crawling and fluid. But my attention is on the carved stone in the man's hand. I see a bloody tuft of tangled hair matted at one corner. Jeremias McCreevey's, I'm sure.

The skell looks up, and his bloodshot eyes widen at my recognition. I gotta wonder what possessed him to carry the murder weapon all through the day, cops on his trail, choppers beating down from the sky. In the distance I can still hear them, but too far away. I wish I was alone, wish Danny could fly to safety. I paw at my waist in search of a weapon which hasn't been there since I retired. The moment stretches. A shred of cloud passes before the sun and a chill runs through me. The fellow hefts the stone, lips peeled back from his rotting teeth. Later, I imagine, Sky 8 will hover overhead. Someone will sit with Luellen in the front room of her house while a team does its work out here, piecing together the last scrap of Mother McCreevey's mess. The pursuit will continue.

"I eat bugs."

The bastard drops his eyes to Danny. I'm sure the world is about to end. But Danny spreads his wings and squeaks. I can't guess what the tweaker sees, looking at my sweet little bat, but he screams and hurls the stone with all his wiry, cranked strength. I throw myself toward Danny, a feckless shield, but the stone arcs harmlessly through the air above us. For a moment I see it framed by the steely sky, then it clatters against the bat roost and lands with a thud in the dirt below. The tweaker runs past us, waving his arms over his head. I watch him disappear up the block, his howl fading.

The energy drains out of me in the space of a heartbeat. I stumble to the stoop and sit. Danny watches, curious for a moment, but then gets back on bat-winged task. I pull out my cell phone and dial a number I know as well as my own. I describe the fellow and the direction he ran. They'll want to collect the weapon too, so I tell them where to find it. I hang up before they can ask my name, though they'll get it when they run my number. Later.

Danny pulls up short at the bottom of the steps, his expression fierce with bug-eating batistry.

"That was something, eh, buddy?"

He gazes at me. Then he points at the next house. He's ready for trick-or-treat. I draw a deep breath and tell him we have to wait for his mom. At that moment Luellen pops out her front door and trots across the street. "How are you boys doing? Anything interesting happen while I was gone?"

Danny is fluttering around the yard again. In the distance, I hear sirens and the chop of rotors drawing near. I start to describe the encounter, but then I note the high color in Luellen's cheeks, see the breeze move her dark hair. She's ready to go, eager to run through the streets with her little boy, to knock on doors and collect treats as the daylight fades and crisp autumn twilight descends.

"He's been eating bugs."

She grins. "Guess what. While I was inside I heard on the news the girl is going to be okay. The baby too. Both are out of danger."

"That's good."

Danny flits over to me and takes my hand. Luellen offers him his pumpkin bucket, its triangle eyes alight, and together we walk down a street made gold by the setting sun.

Dead Line

Pat Dennis

"One hundred and thirty-four goblins! There are one hundred and thirty-four goblins in her yard, not fifteen like she claimed. I counted them," Kate sputtered, her arms folded across the front of her wide body.

Phil lowered his *Maxim* magazine and rested it on his equally broad belly. "You said it was completely dark when you drove by your sister's house. How could you count them?"

Her eyes adjusted into laser beams of hate. "I used my pocket flashlight," she responded in a voice so frigid it momentarily ended global warming.

"Kate, settle down. Puck's your sister, after all. I mean, maybe she wants to be like you? Take it as a compliment."

"Be like me? Puck hates me. She's hated me from the day she was born."

"How's that possible? You're younger than she is."

Kate let out a sigh of married exasperation. "She knew I'd make an appearance—eventually."

Phil's eyebrow shot up in disbelief as he said, "Don't you think you're exaggerating?"

"Me, exaggerating? Am I the one with one hundred and thirty-four goblins? Am I the one going overboard with Halloween do-dads and what-knots?" Kate challenged, her nose pressed against the picture window of her living room. Tomorrow afternoon her front yard would be filled with dozens of pumpkins, witches, bats, miniature haunted castles, ghosts, and life-size ghouls made from filling Phil's old shirts and pants with batting. A stuffed pillowcase tied into a ball for the head, with a baseball cap jauntily sitting on top, would complete the look. And still, all of that wouldn't be enough. Puck's decorations would triple hers.

While using a finger to tap against the cold windowpane, Kate continued, "The deadline for decorating is tomorrow at 6:00 p.m. There's no way I'll win the contest."

"Quality counts, not quantity," Phil comforted, strumming through the advertisements for herbal male enhancement drugs in the back of his men's magazine. "Besides, you've won the city's Best Decorated Halloween House every year you've entered."

"That's because Puck moved away from home for thirty years. Now that she's back I'll never win anything again."

Kate yanked at the drapery's drawstring, shutting out the front yard that she now considered measly and pathetically tossed together.

She stared at her husband of three decades. He'd always been too soft on Puck, never being able to comprehend just how evil her sister really was. Kate decided to try to make him understand Puck's dark side one more time. If she could, it would be easier for her to explain later why she had to do what she had to do.

Through a rigid jaw, she said, "You don't get it. Halloween was always mine. It was the only day I had all year. She owned every other one."

"Uh-huh," Phil nodded, his eyes a mere quarter-inch from the magazine page. As soon as he'd turned fifty last year, her mid-life crisis spouse stopped using reading glasses and started using hair dye.

And now he wasn't paying attention to a single word she was saying. Men!

Kate stormed out of the room. It was useless. Whenever she brought up Puck, Phil would suddenly turn into some sort of a saint, preaching love, forgiveness, and freaking family values.

She headed to the kitchen and opened a cupboard. Ten bags of miniature candy bars purchased for Halloween treats sat on the top shelf. Kate grabbed a bag and headed to her bedroom down the hall to think. She'd long ago moved into the guest bedroom on the lower level to escape Phil's snores. His rattle was so loud it could wake the dead, she'd told him.

By the time Kate lay in her bed with tiny discarded silver candy bar wrappers strewn across her Berber carpeting and nightstand, she knew what needed to be done. And she would do it while the entire world slept.

❖

At 3:00 A.M. Kate was still wide-awake. The chocolate treats in her room were long gone, but the caffeine in her system wasn't. It was time.

She threw back the comforter and stepped out of bed. There was no need to dress because she hadn't taken off her clothes. Her boots stood next to her bed. Her coat, gloves and hat rested on the armchair across the room. Of course there was no reason to be quiet. Phil was not only upstairs, but he could sleep through a tornado while it snatched the house away.

Slipping on her boots, Kate took the time to ruminate on how, except for Halloween, family holidays centered on the precious and ever-perky Puck.

Every Christmas morning Puck dressed up as an elf. She was the one chosen to be Santa's Little Helper and pass out the presents. She was the one who always received the biggest gifts.

Puck took up Irish dancing as well, ruining St. Patty's Day forever for Kate. The first time Puck showed up with bunny ears on Easter morning, Kate threw an oatmeal-filled spoon in her direction. Kate received a spanking for being mean. Not Puck, who should have received one for being a show-off.

Kate slipped on her coat and gloves. It wasn't very cold, but she wanted to make sure that no fingerprints would be left behind. She opened her bedroom door and snuck down the hallway past the family photos she'd inherited. There were photos of Puck dressed up as Lady Liberty or Betsy Ross for 4th of July. At only ten years of age, six years before she even had a job, Puck managed to take over Labor Day as well. She was voted Little Miss Worker and rode on the town's float. The newspaper photo of her was displayed for two million years on their family mantel.

Kate stepped outside and walked toward her garage, her rage growing with every stomp of her foot. She breathed in deep, the crisp air filling her lungs. And, although it was the dead of morning, she could smell the burning leaves of a bonfire.

A pitchfork rested against the side of the garage. Kate grabbed it. She turned and headed down the street, aiming for her sister's house, the same sibling who used to hate Halloween as much as Kate loved it. It hadn't been until Kate discovered Halloween and her sister's innate aversion to all things scary that life became bearable. The young Puck had quivered at the sight of skeletons, mummies and third graders dressed as vampires. Every Halloween morning, she'd lie in her bed, refusing to get up. Her parents would hug her in understanding. She'd cuddle underneath her Barbie-Doll bedspread, surrounded by teddy bears and toy unicorns. Her face would be turned toward the wall and she'd stare at her Bambi poster for comfort.

Meanwhile, on Halloween, on *her* side of the room, Kate would eagerly hop out of bed, tossing back her orange and black bedspread, pushing aside a dozen plush spiders and thirteen black stuffed cats. Excited that her day had finally arrived, she'd reach over and kiss each of the movie posters hanging over her bed. Every single one was an image of a monster from a classic Hollywood movie.

It *was* her day, she grumbled now as she turned the corner onto Elm Street. Decades later, for no apparent reason, it had suddenly become Puck's.

Puck's house was at the end of the block. As Kate walked down the street, her flashlight shone on the decorated yards she passed. A few were done in the preposterous cute look, turning Halloween into a ludicrously happy event of smiling ghosts and grinning pumpkins. Other homeowners had wisely chosen creepy, and cardboard tombstones with fake blood won out over silly, straw-filled scarecrows.

When Kate reached Puck's tri-level at the end of the block, the front yard looked like a warehouse of horrors. It had only been five hours since Kate's last reconnaissance, but she could swear Puck had added even more decorations. There was barely room to walk as Kate crept around to the side of the house, pitchfork in hand.

Of course it had crossed her mind to kill her sister. What sister hasn't had that thought? Especially on Halloween? But she had chosen a different though equally fine plan that would assure her the win as well. Kate would demolish every single decoration in Puck's yard, poking them to Hell with her prong, one by one.

It wasn't until she stabbed the third goblin that she saw him, perched on a tree limb, his chubby body wider than the tree trunk he rested against. A pair of binoculars were positioned in his hands and focused on the second-floor window. Puck's window. Kate's sister was walking around stone-cold naked, her silicone enhanced, thousand-year-old breasts bouncing with each step.

Puck had always been a night owl. But the man in the tree was in bed and sound asleep by 9:00 P.M. Or at least that's what Phil always told her.

In an instant, the disturbing facts of their marriage became crystal clear to Kate. Why Phil had insisted that Puck be her Maid of Honor. Why Phil always stood up for Puck. Why he defended her actions. Why he'd lent Puck money to move back to her hometown after her divorce.

And why he didn't mind at all when Kate moved out of their bedroom.

Phil leaned toward the house, a sly smile on his face. He was wearing tattered old jeans and a plaid flannel shirt. Long thermal underwear peeked out from underneath. On his head rested a Minnesota Twins baseball cap. He still hadn't noticed her standing below, pitchfork in hand.

Kate would always be surprised at how quickly she became protective of her sister. Until that moment, she hadn't understood how deeply bloodlines ran. She lifted her fork and knew if Phil didn't die she'd divorce him.

But die he did. Not from the pitchfork. Kate's weak toss sent it just a few feet in the air. But the surprise of seeing a flying farm implement coming his way caused Phil to fall from his perch. As he did, his head caught between two branches and his neck snapped like a wishbone shared between two kids at Thanksgiving.

Puck didn't win the contest after all. When the body was finally discovered to be real and not a stuffed ghoul, her yard became an official crime scene. The subsequent yellow tape ruled out any prize.

Kate didn't win the contest either. In fact, she didn't even answer her door until that evening when the police came by to inform her that her husband had been accidentally killed. He'd fallen out of a tree it seemed. They regretted to tell her that Phil was a peeper.

But Kate didn't spend Halloween huddled inside her house mourning the loss of her husband. Instead it was spent online, ordering Christmas decorations galore. The life insurance money coming her way would cover the expense.

It was time for a new holiday. A day that celebrated a new beginning, and, eventually, a rebirth. She'd set aside Halloween and concentrate on Santa Claus. A round, cheery man she could actually trust.

Time of Death

David Housewright

A small brick building, one story high and less than thirty feet across, crouched in the middle of the block. It was the police station, although there was no sign that said so. A uniformed sergeant sat behind an old, battered desk. As far as Logan could tell, he was the only man in the station house.

"He'p ya?" the sergeant said.

Logan flashed his ID.

"Yeah, the Chief said you'd be around," the sergeant said. "Come to look at our killer, did you?"

"That's right."

"Pretty little thing. Hard to believe she slashed her boyfriend's throat. 'Course, she denies it."

"I bet she does," Logan said.

"I gotta tell ya…" The sergeant grunted as he lifted his enormous frame from the chair and circled the desk. "I 'spect you see this sorta thing all the time, but a small town like this one, I gotta tell ya, it's the biggest thing ever happened here. Well, second biggest thing. I can understand why the Chief would call in you big-city boys."

The sergeant led Logan to the back of the building. There was a heavy metal door with a small window. The window was made of thick glass crisscrossed with iron threads. Logan looked through the glass. The girl was sitting on the edge of a narrow cot attached to the wall, her head in her hands.

"There she is," the sergeant said. He fitted a key into the lock and gave it a turn. The door swung open. "Want I should stay?"

"That won't be necessary," Logan said. "But I'm expecting a report from the medical examiner. Let me know when it arrives."

"You got it."

Logan stepped into the cell. The sergeant closed the door and locked him in.

"Laurel Clark," Logan said.

The girl looked up. Her eyes were swollen and her cheeks were puffy from crying. She wore her hair in a ponytail tied with a red ribbon, but the ribbon had become loose and Logan figured a firm head shake would send it flying. She rubbed her eyes with the back of her hands and looked up again. Logan decided that there was something extraordinarily touching about her, but quickly pushed the thought from his mind. You know better than that, he told himself.

He let her look at his badge and identification.

"My name is Logan. I'm with the Minnesota Bureau of Criminal Apprehension."

"It's all my fault," she said.

"Ms. Clark, have you been informed of your rights?"

She said she had, but he read them to her again anyway. He asked how old she was.

"Nineteen," she said. Which made her a legal adult. Which meant he did not have to inform her parents before questioning her. If she had said she was sixteen, Logan would have believed her.

"Will you answer some questions for me?" he asked.

"Sure."

"You don't have to. If you want an attorney – "

"It's okay."

"I read the report. It's an amazing story."

"You don't believe me either."

"The report says you had a motive for killing your boyfriend."

"Ex-boyfriend."

"Witnesses say that you were the one who coerced him into the house where he was killed."

"Yes."

"You admitted to the police that you were responsible for your boyfriend's death."

"Ex-boyfriend. Tommy was my ex-boyfriend. And I said I was responsible. I didn't say I actually killed him."

"Where were you when he was killed?"

"I was at home in bed."

"Any witnesses?"

"At 2:15 A.M.?" Laurel smiled slightly. "No, there weren't any witnesses."

"In what way were you responsible for your boy—excuse me—ex-boyfriend's death?"

"You said you read the report."

"I'd like to hear the story in your own words."

Laurel sighed deeply and rubbed her eyes again. "Do you believe in ghosts, Mr. Logan?"

"No."

"I do. I believe in ghosts. I didn't believe until last night. I believe now."

"Tell me about it."

"There's a farmhouse out on the county road about ten miles from town. The old Utley place."

"The place where Tommy's body was found?" Logan said.

Laurel nodded.

❖

She was ten when Delores Utley died and even now it was hard to take. Delores had been the girl Laurel had most looked up to, had most wanted to be like. She was smart and she was lovely and she could dance—Delores was the best dancer in Mrs. Cummings' Dance School. Laurel had gone to all of her recitals, and because Delores danced, Laurel wanted to dance. But more important, Delores always treated Laurel like an equal, like a friend. She never said, "This is the kid I sometimes baby-sit." Instead, Delores would give her a hug or slap her hand in greeting and tell her high-school classmates, "Meet my friend, Laurel."

And then she died. The day after Halloween they found her in the Utley home hanging from a rope she had tied herself. At her feet was her boyfriend, his throat slashed so deeply that his head hung backward like the hood of a sweatshirt. According to local gossip, the boyfriend had convinced Delores that he loved her, had taken her virginity, and then discarded her. She begged him to come back. He not only refused, he flaunted his new girlfriend in front of her. The police called it murder-suicide, although they never did find the weapon that killed the boy.

The Utleys moved away from the house and it had remained vacant all those years. Rumors circulated that it was haunted. Laurel never believed the rumors. Yet she could not pass the abandoned house without feeling unbearably sad.

Her childhood friend Tommy, however, did believe the rumors. He even claimed to have seen a young woman dressed in white passing before the windows late at night on a number of occasions. Once, when he mustered enough courage to investigate, he said that he came close enough to the house to hear Delores weeping over her lost love. But then he laughed and one never knew if he was serious or not.

By the time they were seniors in high school, Laurel and Tommy had stopped being friends and had become something so much more. Laurel still didn't know how it happened, how they had evolved from boy and girl playing in the backyard to man and woman playing in the bedroom. But she remembered one incident in particular that occurred early in their new relationship.

"Remember Delores Utley?" Tommy had asked her. They were naked in Tommy's bedroom, the house empty except for them.

"Of course."

"She was always looking out for you when we were kids. It was understood if you mess with Laurel you answer to Delores."

"I remember."

"After we started dating, she came to me in a dream. She said I should be good to you or else."

"Or else what?"

"She didn't say, but I remember what happened to her boyfriend."

Laurel thought it was a wonderful lie and poked Tommy in the ribs.

"Don't do that," Tommy said. He rolled out of bed and stared down at her. Sweat beaded on his forehead and his body seemed to tremble. "I'm not kidding. She came to me in a dream. More than one dream. She was serious."

It was then that Laurel knew. Tommy really was afraid of ghosts, especially the ghost of Delores Utley.

"Better be nice to me then," she said.

Only Tommy hadn't been nice to her. He professed his undying love for Laurel the night they first made love and then again the night before she left for college in September. But by the time she returned home for Halloween, he was sleeping with Tiffany Brent who was still in high school. Laurel was stunned by this development and reminded him that he was the only man she had known. He responded by asking how long he was supposed to wait for her.

"More than eight weeks," she told him.

The day after Halloween there was a party—beer and a bonfire at the lake. All the kids home from college and those who had stayed in the little town were there. Tommy told stories, as he always did, while Tiffany stared adoringly at him.

"Tommy's afraid of ghosts," Laurel said. That caused several heads to turn. "I mean it. He's terrified of Delores Utley. He claims she comes to him in his dreams. Isn't that right, Tommy?"

"You're crazy," Tommy said.

"How 'bout it, Tiff?" Laurel said. "Has Tommy ever mentioned his fear of ghosts to you?"

Tiffany did the worst thing she could have done to her man. She looked him in the eye and said, "Is it true?"

After that, Laurel didn't have to add much to the conversation to keep it going in the direction she wanted. Eventually, Tommy agreed to spend an entire night in the Utley house if that was what it would take to prove his manhood. He was quite surprised when Laurel jumped up and announced, "No time like the present."

"Now?" he said. As someone correctly noted, it was ten years to the day that Delores had killed her boyfriend and hung herself.

"Right now."

Tommy's fear of being ridiculed was far greater than his fear of the grisly anniversary. He allowed Laurel and a dozen friends to escort him to the house where he bravely kissed Tiffany goodbye, said "See you in hell" to the cheering crowd, and entered the house. Most of the kids lingered to see if he tried to escape; a few tossed rocks on the roof and raked tree branches along the walls. They could hear Tommy shouting from inside, "Real funny, guys." After an hour or so, everyone left.

Early the next morning, Tiffany went to the house to see if Tommy was still there or if he had gone home after the crowd dissipated. She found him, dead, his throat slashed, under the beam where Delores Utley had hung herself a decade earlier. Shortly after, the police questioned Laurel.

❖

"I wanted Delores to kill him," she said. "I was desperate for her to kill him but I never really believed that she would."

Laurel covered her face with her hands. "What have I done?"

Logan watched her intently as he leaned against the wall, his arms folded across his chest. He didn't believe her story. His gut and 20 years of experience convinced him that Laurel killed Tommy and set it up so the more gullible would blame Delores Utley. Only he couldn't prove it. The preliminary report he had read earlier said the crime scene investigators were unable to find the murder weapon just as they had been unable to locate it in the first killing. Nor could they uncover a shred of evidence to suggest that anyone had been in the Utley house except Tommy. The case was so weak, Logan was sure if Laurel had asked for an attorney when one had been offered, he would have screamed for her release long before now and he would have gotten it.

Laurel looked up at Logan, studied his expression.

"What will they do to me?" she said.

Logan had no answer. Even if the county attorney believed that the girl had deliberately manipulated Tommy into the house so that Delores would kill him—God, now even he was considering the possibility—what could he do about it? Charge Laurel with conspiracy to commit murder? Call Delores to the stand as a corroborating witness?

The sergeant rapped on the cell door.

"The medical examiner's report just arrived," he said.

Logan excused himself and left the cell. He returned to the front desk and started reading the findings of the Office of the County Coroner. The sergeant glanced at the report over his shoulder.

"So," he said. "Did you hear the girl's story?"

"I heard it."

"What do you think? Do you believe a ghost did it?"

"Do you?"

"You gotta admit, it certainly would make for a novel defense should the matter ever go to trial. Think we'd get on *Court TV?*"

Logan smiled. He held the report up for the sergeant to see and pointed at the line that read Date and Time of Death.

"I don't believe in ghosts," he said. "Do you want to know what I believe in? I believe in forensic pathology."

A minute later Logan was back in the cell standing before the girl.

"Ms. Clark, I would like to clarify something you said earlier," he said.

"Certainly."

"I asked where you were when Tommy was killed."

"I said I was in bed."

"I asked if there were witnesses."

"I said there weren't any."

"No, you said at 2:15 AM there weren't any witnesses."

"So?"

Logan held up the coroner's report. He was smiling broadly. "How did you know that's when Tommy was killed?"

Laurel didn't hesitate for a moment.

"Because Mr. Logan," she said, "2:15—that's the exact same time when Delores Utley killed her boyfriend ten years ago."

World's Greatest Dad

Stephen Blackmoore

By the time Franklin Delacorte wakes up, he's been dead six hours.

He's confused, disoriented. Wondering why he's naked and surrounded by multi-colored candles in the middle of a crypt.

He sits up, wobbles a bit. Steadies himself on the top of the stone sarcophagus he's been lying on. Yellow light gutters through the room, throwing scattered shadows along the stone wall.

The candles are a little unnerving. Scented. Vanilla, spice, potpourri. It smells like his grandmother's house.

"Dude," someone says behind him. "You so have to see this."

Franklin looks to the door at a vaguely familiar teenager. Can't quite place him. Pimples, greasy hair, wearing an old army jacket. A cigarette dangles on the kid's bottom lip, his mouth hanging open. After a moment the cigarette falls to the floor.

"What, did he catch fire?" Another teen comes in beside the first, hitching up his pants and zipping his fly. Too occupied to notice Franklin.

"No, I didn't," Franklin says, freezing the kid mid-step. Apparently, the kid hadn't finished outside. A dark stain spreads through the front of his jeans.

"You're dead," the second kid says.

Takes a second for that to register. And even then it doesn't. Dead? A little wheezy, maybe. Wonders if he's coming down with something. Then his memory kicks in. Who the kids are, robbing the liquor store, guy behind the counter with a shotgun.

He looks down at his stomach, sees the massive hole and scatter the buckshot made. That would explain the wheeze. And also what the kid just said.

He looks up at them, his face hard. "The fuck did you two do this time?"

❖

Franklin's boys are ambitious. Crazy. Stupid sometimes, even. But ambitious.

"And you just raised the dead," Franklin says. "Just like that." He looks from one to the other. They won't meet his eyes.

He turns a dog-eared paperback in his hands titled *Go Satan!* in bright red letters that look like dripping blood. The tag line below it reads, *Learn To Pick Up Girls With The Dark Arts!*

"Sorry," Billy says, hands thrust deep in the pockets of his army jacket.

"Didn't think it would work," says Jake, still scrubbing his sleeve at the embarrassing stain on his jeans.

Franklin flips pages to a chapter titled "Bring 'Em Back Alive! Stuff To Do on the Day of the Dead" and reads a few lines.

The book tells him it's a good thing he died on Halloween. He thinks it would have been better if he hadn't died at all.

"Whose idea was this?" he says.

They both point at each other.

Franklin shakes his head. "Fine. Whatever. Did you at least think to bring me some pants?"

They give each other that "Oh, yeah," look they get whenever they figure out something tricky. Like tying their shoes.

Franklin shakes his head. "Tell me you at least drove me here."

❖

Franklin sits in the back of Billy's broken-down Cougar, the body bag from the morgue wrapped around his waist. The Cougar would be a classic car if it wasn't mostly rust with an engine that sounds like a wood chipper. Billy keeps working on it, but it never seems to get any better.

"This is what I get for busting my butt to keep you boys out of trouble. Didn't you learn a thing in Sunday school? Like don't play with the forces of the devil?"

"Jeez, Dad, we said we were sorry," Jake says.

Franklin's a little worried. He's seen movies. He knows how this sort of thing turns out. "I don't even want to know how you did it, but I swear if I get an urge to gnaw on some brains I'm gonna start with yours."

The robbery at the liquor store should have gone off without a hitch. Figured it being Halloween he could walk in with a mask on and no one would bat an eyelash until he was all the way to the cash register.

The guy behind the counter had other ideas. Shot Franklin before he could even get his gun out of his waistband.

He looks at the garbage cluttering the backseat. Finds some rags Billy's been using to clean up oil and gasoline as he works on his car. Better than nothing. He stuffs them into the hole in his stomach.

So what to do now? Well, find some pants. But after that?

Franklin's slowly coming to accept being dead. Hard to argue with a four-inch hole in your gut that doesn't bleed so much as ooze. He looks down at his feet. It's hard to tell in the momentary flash of streetlights going by, but he thinks they might be turning purple. He remembers something about blood pooling.

Should he stand on his head for a while?

He thinks about what zombies do. They eat people. He knows that much. But he's more in the mood for a Big Mac. He looks at the oily rags holding his guts in. Maybe not.

Whatever this is, he's not dead. Not really. What if this is a second chance? A chance to make things better. For him, for his boys.

"When's the last you boy's seen your mother?"

They exchange glances. "Week ago," Billy says.

"You don't want to eat her brains, do you?" Jake says.

"No," he says, though the idea did occur to him. "I want to make amends."

❖

"This is an awful bad idea, Dad," Jake says. His finger is hovering over the doorbell to their mom's small, one bedroom bungalow, a Lexus in the driveway.

Quiet, tree-lined street. Late, but not so late that there aren't at least a handful of trick-or-treaters still out scrounging for the last of the Jujubes or maybe a Snickers.

"Trust your father, boys, I know what I'm doing."

Only he doesn't. He hasn't seen Pearl in over two years. He didn't know she'd moved out of her apartment into a nice part of town.

He'd had the boys stop in at a Walmart and grab him some clothes. A pair of sweatpants and a hoodie. They didn't have any cash and couldn't figure out a way to hide shoes in Billy's jacket.

Standing out here in bare feet, ill-fitting clothes and dead doesn't give him a lot of confidence. But he'll be damned if he lets the boys see that.

Franklin slaps Jake on the back. "Well, go on, do it."

Jake sighs, closes his eyes, pushes the button. A moment later the door swings open to a man in a polo shirt, chinos and a wolfman mask yelling, "Booga booga."

Instead of the trick-or-treat Franklin had ready on his lips, he comes out with, "Who the fuck are you?"

The man pulls the mask off to better see Franklin and spots the boys.

"Oh," he says connecting the dots. Looks Franklin up and

down. "You must be Franklin. Evening, boys."

"Evening, sir," they say together.

"Doesn't answer my question," Franklin says, but the man is ignoring him, so he turns to the boys. "You never call me sir."

"Pearl," the man calls out behind him. "It's for you." He steps aside. "Come on in. Might as well get this over with."

❖

The five of them sit in Pearl's living room. Franklin eyes the glass cases full of porcelain figurines and Beanie Babies with suspicion. Wonders about the pastel blue furniture from the Sears catalog. There is no sound but the heavy ticking of a grandfather clock.

Pearl looks a little stiff. She's wearing a skirt, a blouse with a high collar and no cleavage, sensible-looking Mary Janes. She's gotten them all drinks. Lemonade. Not a hint of vodka. This isn't how he remembers her.

"Franklin," she says, breaking the long stretch of silence. "You're looking…good."

"Oh, don't lie to him," the man next to her says. He turns to Franklin, sticks out his hand to shake. "You look like you've been shit through a rhinoceros. Name's Lawrence. Larry to my friends. You can call me Lawrence."

Franklin takes the hand, shakes it. He's more confused than when he woke up dead.

"So," Lawrence says, taking back his hand and wiping it on his chinos. "I suppose you're here about the wedding."

"Wedding?"

"Yes, Franklin," Pearl says, playing with a fold of her skirt. "We're getting married. This July. The boys said they were going to tell you."

"I'm actually kind of surprised you came by," Lawrence says. "The boys told us you'd been shot and killed in a liquor store robbery."

"We thought it was a sick joke," Pearl says.

"I laughed," Lawrence adds. He puts a proprietary arm around Pearl's shoulders.

"Look, here's the thing," Pearl says. "The boys tell us what you're up to. It's not good."

"You're a deadbeat," Lawrence says. "You've done time. You're a bad influence on the boys."

"Now, wait a minute," Franklin says, but Pearl puts a hand up to stop him.

"No, Franklin. Larry and I are getting married and we're giving the boys a good home. I don't want them seeing you anymore. You're bad for them the way you were bad for me."

This isn't going the way Franklin expected at all. Not exactly sure what he was hoping for, but it sure as hell wasn't this.

It's gone all wrong before he's even had a chance to start.

"And the way I hear it," Lawrence says, "you were pretty bad for her. Especially in the sack."

"Boys," Franklin says, standing. Cold rage bubbles up inside him. "Wait in the car."

❖

Franklin comes out an hour later wearing a pair of too tight bicycle shorts and a snow parka. Nothing else of Lawrence's fits and there's no way Franklin can wear his hoodie and sweat pants. There's too much blood on them.

At first he thought he'd have trouble getting into the whole eating brains thing, but once he chewed through Lawrence's skull, the rest was easy. He had a twinge or two about Pearl, but he got over it.

He looks up and down the street. The trick-or-treaters are gone, the June Cleaver houses all buttoned up for the night. He wonders what the neighbors will think when they find the bodies.

He can hear the steady rumble of Billy's Cougar down the block. Now, why'd they park all the way down there?

He gets his answer a second later when the engine revs,

the headlights burst to life, and the car burns rubber as it roars down the street.

Right at Franklin.

The way you kill a zombie, Franklin remembers, is shooting it in the head. He's not sure what a 1968 Mercury Cougar with a 225 horsepower V8 engine driven by a pissed-off teenager will do to him, but he'd really rather not find out.

Franklin runs, though he knows it's no contest. He looks behind him, the wood-chipper roar of the car on his heels just as the Cougar slams into him, bouncing him onto the hood. The windshield cracks as his head smacks against it.

He feels his left arm break, his skull fracture. He's surprised when it doesn't hurt. Then elated. Then pissed off.

He grabs a windshield wiper and holds on, turns himself to face the two boys, Billy at the wheel, Jake white-knuckling the dashboard. Their eyes are wide with terror.

"That does it," Franklin says. "I am gonna give you boys a whuppin' you ain't never gonna forget."

He slams his head hard against the broken windshield. The spider web cracks widen. He's yelling obscenities. The boys are screaming. The car caroms across streets, shrieks up a ramp onto the interstate.

One or two more punches, Franklin figures, he'll break through the glass and really go to town. He pulls back his fist just as Billy yanks the steering wheel hard to the right.

Franklin goes airborne. Watches the lights of the Cougar in the distance surrounded by the smoke of brakes and tires.

He hits the ground, leaving a furrow through grass and dirt as he tumbles like a cannonball. He stops only when he butts up hard against a slab of concrete.

He's really done a number on himself this time. His left arm is completely useless, broken in five, maybe six places. Most of his teeth are scattered behind him. His right leg is twisted at an angle that shouldn't be possible.

Half his tongue is missing.

He pulls himself up anyway. Wobbles a bit. Steadies himself on the tombstone that finally stopped his flight.

He looks around, eyes blurry. He shoves a finger into one of his eyeballs, seating it back into place, and his vision clears.

Where are those little bastards?

He sees them running from the Cougar into the graveyard. Running toward the only light in the place. Toward the crypt he woke up in.

❖

"Come on boys," Franklin says, his voice carrying in the empty graveyard. "Daddy's not gonna hurt ya. Much."

His right leg is worse than he thought. It keeps snagging on the uneven ground, tripping him up. He stopped trying to lift it before he got ten feet. It kept throwing off his balance.

The boys run out of the crypt, Billy with a vanilla scented candle and his copy of *Go Satan!* in his hand, Jake with a bag that's flopping around like it's got a life of its own.

"That's enough, Dad," Billy says. "We brought you back. The least you could have done was not eat mom."

Franklin stops mid-shuffle. Billy's got a point. They did go to a lot of trouble to raise him from the dead. Yeah, he thinks, they hid that their mom was getting married. And they did try to kill him again.

But what did he expect? They're still good boys. They mean well.

"Or Larry," Jake says. "Larry was cool."

Cool? "I'm gonna twist your pea head off your goddamn shoulders, you little sonsabitches," Franklin says. His voice is muddled with only half a tongue, but he gets the point across.

Billy starts reciting from the book, shakes the candle around, spins in a circle. Franklin can't understand any of the words, but it sounds important.

It dawns on him what his son is doing. Sending him back

to the grave. Franklin shuffles forward, dragging his broken leg behind him.

He feels a tugging on the back of his mind. His thoughts slipping. Vision fading round the edges. He stumbles. Arms and legs go numb.

"Now," Billy yells.

Jake grabs the end of the sack he's holding and flings the contents right at Franklin's head. A wailing shriek echoes off the tombstones. A blur of motion smacks Franklin full in the face. He flails at it, screams. Bats it away as it rips long furrows in his flesh.

"The cat was supposed to be dead, you idiot," Billy says.

"Dude, I can't kill a cat."

Franklin's broken arm is tangled up in the snow parka, but the feeling of fading away, of dying all over again, is gone. He surges forward, tearing the parka off.

He's fast for a dead man with a busted leg. And while the boys are bickering, he gets close enough to grab Billy by the arm.

Startled, Billy throws the book at Franklin's cat-mangled face, punches him in the gut with the hand holding the candle. Franklin laughs.

Until the candle lights the oil-and-gasoline-soaked rags he'd stuffed into the shotgun wound.

The rags erupt. Franklin stares at the sudden flames. By the time he figures out what's happening the rags are an inferno in his gut.

He lets go of Billy, slaps at the rags to put the fire out. Instead the wad loosens, hangs out of the hole. The flames spread to his Lycra bicycle shorts.

Franklin loses his shit. One thing to have a gunshot wound, broken bones, missing teeth. Something else entirely to have your dick on fire. The air fills with the stink of burnt hair, cooking meat, melting plastic.

So focused on the flames he doesn't notice the shovel coming right at him.

❖

"He looks awful pissed," Jake says, sitting on top of an abandoned washing machine covered in rust. The dump's not the best-smelling place in town, but nobody comes out here.

"Shoulda just buried him," Billy says.

It's a pretty big jar. They lucked out when they found it. No lid, though. They've got a hubcap on the top to keep the rain out.

"But this is lots cooler," Jake says.

Franklin's head sits on the bottom of the jar, jaw working furiously, eyes bouncing around like they're ping pong balls. Up, down, side to side. Irises are milked over, skin a mottled gray.

Billy raps on the glass. Franklin's wobbly eyes stop, stare at him in cold, hard hatred.

"Yeah," he says, "Lots cooler."

Troubled Water

Heather Dearly

The crowd gathered on Cemetery Road.

Anya Madjigijik—Magik to the locals—watched the implacable flock through a dusty web of white lace curtains. Every year since the tragedy, when the leaves turned to shades of fire and blood, the town crossed the water to mourn. They carried grave flowers for the dead father and his dead daughter, and unrepentant torches of blame for the widow with the weird name.

Anya could remember when her child carried a pail of candy across that bridge.

Could they?

Sipping a still warm tisane, she rose from her wooden rocker and gingerly moved the panel aside. Anya cast a stare on each breathing soul, willing them to remember and see truth. But her futile attempt faded against double-paned glass. Their hearts and eyes were sealed.

"You drink the same water."

The incorporeal voice startled her and Anya lost her hold on vintage lace and hope. Tiny particles spun in the air around her, desperation settling in their place.

"No…. My water is clean." She choked out the words past bits of spit and fear, gripping her teacup to avoid a spill.

She'd met the traveler the summer he wore human skin and breathed the air of mortals. His borrowed face bore unsightly scars and her husband had taken pity on him, allowing him to help dig plots, wash headstones, and assist with maintenance in exchange for three squares and a cot in the original caretaker's residence. Power and water had been turned off in the old hovel, an expense they could not afford. Mr. Magik had offered use of their indoor shower to the man who called himself Byron Dodd, but he had refused.

He'd bathed himself after dark under the bridge.

The night before the accident, Anya caught sight of his skin from her kitchen window. His bone-pale flesh reflected a warm golden glow, a haunting beacon in the moonlit sparkling waters of new autumn. A switch of consciousness flipped inside her that night and for the first time in three months she knew exactly what he was.

The next morning she asked him to leave. And when Byron Dodd crossed the bridge that afternoon, he took her husband and daughter's last breaths with him. But he didn't take the blame. He left the blame with her.

"Your resistance is amusing."

Her grip loosened and porcelain shattered at her feet.

"Do you ever ask yourself why their Guardians left them for me to steal? Do you wonder why your Watcher remains?"

The Memitim's voice was hollow and left an unwelcome chill in the room. And yes, she'd wondered why her Guardian Angel remained by her side when her husband and daughter had been the modern-day saints. Anya was rumored a witch at worst and an atheist at best. She'd never labeled herself as either, but her childhood faith had worn thin as a toothpick by the time Byron Dodd arrived, only to return full of splinters after she'd lost everything that mattered.

"I want you to leave." She would not concede to the messenger of death.

"I'll be back."

And in the fading haze of his presence, the answer to why she remained under the care of an angel became clear as water. The certainty of what she must do flooded her soul, breaching her sorrow with new direction.

Widow Magik would rinse this life away.

Anya shook chips of white off her feet as she reached for the wrap hanging on the wrought-iron rack by the front door. After covering herself in crocheted warmth, she left her home without reservation, facing those in front of her for the last time as their goat.

Hushed whispers swirled in the sky like hungry vultures as she walked past breathing bodies to bid final farewell to the dead. The earth covering her family's remains was hallowed ground as far as she was concerned, and the crowd was staining it with their presence.

"They are not yours to grieve; they are mine," she said. "They will always be mine."

And if the crowd refused to accept the truth, they would become hers, too.

She knelt on damp soil, her hands wiping cold, flat markers free of nature's debris as she leaned over each slice of marble to kiss the names GRIGORY and LARA. There was no engraved ANYA because Anya was meant for something else.

Something beyond her own grave.

Anya rushed toward the road where the trouble began, to where it would end and begin again filtered and fresh. There would be no fear, no pain—only purpose, impending balance, and peace.

The land sloped down to the stream, an uneven ramp beneath her feet. Careful steps carried her to the edge of the bank, and that's when she saw it—her reflection, a shimmering ivory absence of life. Leaning in closer, she could see her skeleton beneath her skin and angel wings wrapped around her bones; her guardian wishing her well and goodbye, silently encouraging her to walk into the water and claim her right to immortality.

She dove in alone.

Reaching beneath stones and gritty river bottom, Anya retrieved what had belonged to her all along. Byron Dodd had bathed in the water beneath the bridge because he'd been searching for the one thing that could bring him legitimacy, but he never found what he was looking for. He'd never found her scythe.

And Byron Dodd would never steal a soul before its time again.

Anya Magik emerged from the water with her destiny in hand. The crowd saw the wet, shivering widow with her arm raised high and it looked as if she were waving an imaginary flag of white, begging for a truce. It wasn't time for them to see what she was really carrying with her until it was their time to go to a land beyond troubled water, but they did see sadness washed from her eyes and their hearts softened.

They saw the true face of Magik.

And it was beautiful.

Friday Night Dining with Marianne

Mark Hull

"See ya, Hazel. Have a good weekend!"

So said a coworker to me on his way out the door late one Friday. My name is Marianne Hazlitt, and I think that my coworkers call me Hazel in an attempt to endear themselves to me. That attempt fails. I hate my coworkers.

I work for a large newspaper in Greater Los Angeles, the name of which is unimportant. I am a food critic there, the junior of two that the newspaper employs. The senior food critic is Arthur Earl, and he could not tell *crêpes suzette* from Susanne Pleshette in a brightly lit room even if they both bore clearly-spelled placards with their respective names on them. That is my own little joke about Mr. Earl.

But humor aside, I strongly feel that both my taste and my writing are superior to Mr. Earl's in every way. The newspaper editorial staff is singularly unenlightened, however, so I suppose I shall have to wait until Mr. Earl is no longer with us to become the senior food critic here. That day will not come soon enough to suit me. I hate Mr. Earl.

Every Friday I dine at a different *restaurant de haute cuisine* (which, in French, means "restaurant of fine dining") in this godforsaken city, and write about the experience the following week in a serial column I call "Friday Night Dining with Marianne." This particular Friday I'd reserved a table (under an assumed name, of course) at a restaurant called L'Homme in Bel Air. The reservation was not until later in the evening, so I took a taxi home from work and luxuriated in a well-deserved bath before dressing for dinner.

It happened to be Halloween as well as a Friday, and I was grateful for a reason not to be at home when the neighborhood urchins came begging for the garbage they call candy. They have not in the past seemed to appreciate overmuch the broccoli and photocopied articles on healthy eating that I have given them, the ungrateful wretches, so for all I cared they could pass this Halloween in ignorance with rotting teeth, dyspepsia and gout. I hate them. And their parents, for that matter.

Eventually I called a taxicab and left for my dinner reservation. It had become an atramentous and tempestuous evening, and I must confess that I was quite drenched after sprinting from my door to the cab. This dampened my spirits considerably, and I was no longer in as gay a mood as had been the case in the bathtub earlier. The cab driver, a foreign gentleman, seemed unclear as to the location of L'Homme, so I had to enunciate the directions to the restaurant several times, and more than once correct him when he took a wrong turn. I find cab drivers so tiresome in this accursed city. In fact I often find myself hating them.

I arrived at the restaurant at last. The taxi driver became quite rude when I did not give him a tip, or at least I so inferred even though I could not understand the language in which he muttered. I shall never tip for poor service, however; that is a rule upon which I am quite firm. Eventually he drove off. I hate him.

The outside of L'Homme was unprepossessing, to say the least. However, I resolved to give the restaurant a fair chance, for I am first and foremost a journalist, and I must upon occasion bear up under adversity in the name of my profession. But I digress. The exterior of L'Homme was somewhat dimly lit, but it appeared to be a restaurant of fine dining as I had been led to believe; and I was much encouraged at the sight of a gentleman entering said establishment dressed for both the evening and the weather in a billowing dark cape with a scarlet lining.

The building itself was made of brick, which appeared to have been recently painted a reddish ochre, and, with the wind, the sign proclaiming the name of the restaurant creaked as it swung back and forth. I made a mental note to mention this annoying squeak to the management, since it is upon these seemingly innocuous things that the fate of even the best restaurant hangs.

Looking more closely, it appeared that L'Homme possessed no windows facing the street; however, I quickly forgave them this flaw as I realized that quite possibly this neighborhood had a problem with panhandlers and such. I felt it quite likely that the proprietors did not want their diners to be forced to observe such riffraff as they enjoyed their meals, a sentiment with which I heartily agreed.

In spite of the driving rain, I endeavored to read the restaurant's posted menu before entering; however, this was made quite difficult by the flickering streetlight on the corner. As I stood there, I imagined that I heard a large animal, quite likely a dog, howl in the distance. No sooner had the howl trailed off than I was convinced I heard a woman scream from much nearer. Here I must confess that I briefly felt a *frisson* of fear, for Bel Air is not the nicest of cities, so I gave up trying to read the menu and entered the restaurant proper.

"*Bonsoir, madame,* and welcome to L'Homme. Do you have a reservation with us this evening?" was the supercilious greeting I received from the *maître d'hôtel* in the foyer, and because of this I immediately began to hate him. The man was middle aged, had a slight paunch, was attired poorly for his position, and his *faux* French accent was atrocious. I was, however, quite certain that he could have fooled Mr. Earl into thinking he was a Frenchman. Mr. Earl is a cretin and I hate him.

"Indeed I do," I replied. "I am Dorothy Donner, and I have a reservation for eight o'clock. I shall be dining alone this evening." Dorothy Donner was the *nom de gastronomie* I had chosen for the evening, of course. It is at this point in my culinary adventures that I am sometimes recognized for who I am because of the small image of Yours Truly that appears each week next to "Friday Night Dining with Marianne." However, I must also add that the photograph I mention is *most* unflattering and I hate both it and the man who took it, even though that man is no longer with us.

The *maître d'* consulted a ledger on his stand and ostentatiously pronounced that he did in fact have an eight o'clock reservation for me, yet since it was only 7:35 he was very sorry but there would be a brief wait for a table. He must have sensed that I was miffed at this shabby treatment for he also said that, because it was Halloween, they were extremely busy and must therefore be slightly less accommodating than would otherwise be the case.

I had no idea what difference it being Halloween made, but I did not at that time choose to ask him, so I walked over and seated myself in the foyer. The décor of the restaurant seemed to consist of antique oil paintings of ferocious-looking gentlemen, dark red walls, chandeliers and the occasional arras. I carefully recorded that fact in a small notebook that I carry for this purpose. I also observed that there were seemingly no mirrors in the restaurant, which I found odd because the aforementioned *motif* is of course all about ornate gilt mirrors. I noted this as well.

Eventually I came to examine the couple in the foyer whom I presumed were also waiting for a table. The gentleman was a bit hirsute for my taste, but was at least attired properly in coat and tails. I could not help but notice, however, that the elbows and knees of his raiment were torn in a manner suggesting that his body had but that very evening undergone a marked transformation in size, a ludicrous thought that caused me to promptly chastise myself for frivolity. I did also note in passing that he appeared to be from London, judging by his strong accent. I have always found the British to be most annoying and I hate them.

The woman, his companion, was likewise attired correctly for the evening, but I cannot say that I approved of her hairstyle. The "big hair" with wavy streaks of white along the side went out of fashion long ago, although I must admit that I did fondly recall having a similar hair style when I attended prom my senior year at school. However, the boy that took me was a pig. I hated him then and I hate him still.

At last, having seated the waiting couple, the *maître d'* came into the foyer and announced "Donner, party of one" in quite an inappropriately loud voice. Was it my imagination, or did I hear him snicker after his announcement? I considered remonstrating with him since I was the only one remaining to be seated, but I decided against it lest I sound priggish. I did, however, enter it into my notebook as I began to hate him in earnest.

Once I was seated at a reasonably good table—after having to explain more than once to the *maître d'* what a reasonably good table was, and why I should be seated at one—I examined the menu.

At this point, in the interest of good journalism, I am forced to admit that occasionally, while dining out, I am subject to that feminine complaint so charmingly called by the French "*flatulence des anges.*" This occasion was one of those times, and as I began to peruse the menu I noticed several people in nearby tables glance at me at first in disbelief, then in horror. I reminded myself that there are boors everywhere and ignored them as best I could, and of course I hated them intensely.

Eventually the *sommelier* came to my table, and during an extended conference I made it clear to him that I was no neophyte when it came to *le vin*. The *sommelier* eventually recommended a Spanish red called "Sangre de Los Bebés," and I followed his recommendation; this in spite of the fact that I had already determined I hated the *sommelier* for his insolence. The wine was a deep ruby color and had a youngish nose; the lingering finish had a bit too much iron in it for my taste; and it had a tendency to clot; but in spite of these small details and much to my own surprise I quite enjoyed it overall, and I resolved to seek out more bottles of the same if I could but find them. The *sommelier* was skeptical that I would be so fortunate as that, but he encouraged me to try if I liked the "Sangre" that much.

Shortly after the visit from the *sommelier*, the *maître d'* must have regretted his earlier impertinence because he came to my table and suggested that he order for me, "as he could see that *madame*, though perhaps previously unacquainted with the *cuisine* of L'Homme, was certainly no stranger to fine dining, and *madame* most definitely merited the special attention of her *maître d'hôtel*, who, he had not thought to mention earlier, was also the owner of this humble establishment."

Though normally immune to such flattery, I must say that I began at last to feel that I would get the service that I deserved, and my mood brightened somewhat. I suspect the wine also helped to mellow me, as an exceptional red will sometimes do. In fact this may well have been the case, since I was forced to belatedly wipe with my napkin a trickle of ruby wine that dripped from the side of my mouth.

I was first presented, as a compliment of the house, a delightful *amuse-bouche* that the *maître d'* had *chef* prepared especially for me. He explained that it was a Sherpa delicacy and that its colorful name, when literally translated, meant "mountaineer's eyeball in aspic." While it was true that it did look something like a human eyeball, I found that it also strongly resembled one of the exceptionally large grapes that are grown in the Loire Valley, both in texture and in taste. The tartness of the aspic set it off quite nicely as well, I thought.

When I asked that he convey my own compliments on the *amuse-bouche* to the chef, the *maître d'* smiled and replied that he would do so. *Chef* would be most pleased, he said, particularly since mountaineers are so difficult to obtain in Los Angeles around the Halloween season. I found myself tittering like a schoolgirl at his joke, even though I was still a bit unsure about the Halloween part. "To heck with it," I said to myself at this point, and I ordered another bottle of the "Sangre de Los Bebés."

The next course to be served consisted of a small garden salad of red lettuce and radicchio, dressed with what the *maître d'* called "Soylent Green," and sprinkled with sea monkeys. The dressing to which he referred was indeed a brilliant green, and had bits of what I took to be bacon in it. The dressing had an unusual taste that I had difficulty identifying, but the smokiness of the bits of bacon combined nicely with its pungency. I was beginning to become impressed with L'Homme, and even, quite to my own astonishment, hating the *maître d'* less.

The next course presented to me was an entrée that, when prepared properly, is perhaps my favorite: *saltimbocca.* L'Homme's version was most definitely prepared properly, and was moist, tender and wonderfully piquant, and I said as much to the *maître d'*. He smiled broadly at that, though he maintained that the veal was not veal at all, but was instead a chubby Boy Scout.

The *maître d'* glanced around, then leaned closer toward me. "The Boy Scout," he explained quietly, "is put through a closely-guarded secret process consisting of bastinado, decollation, defenestration, lapidation, and vapulation before being rolled up and cooked with Marsala and butter, which was why it is so tender."

I found this to be nearly unintelligible after my third bottle of wine—did I fail to mention I had ordered a third?—but I remained silent because some mystery surrounding a work of culinary art like this was, I felt, not a bad thing. Mr. Earl might not agree with me on this, but Mr. Earl is an ass.

The penultimate dish to be served was to be a Southern favorite called hoecake, but I had to insist that I could not eat this and still have room for dessert. That was fine, he said, and "between *madame* and himself the local hoes were not as good this time of year as they were in the spring."

Dessert apparently presented something of a dilemma to the *maître d'*. He said he had difficulty in choosing between Baked Alaskan and ladyfingers drizzled with a raspberry-chocolate sauce. He finally decided to go with the ladyfingers, because he said that at L'Homme, they weren't "lady" fingers at all but were instead the ring fingers of virgins who had died of broken hearts and were quite difficult to find at any price.

"I can imagine," I said as I crunched on one. Strangely, at this point I felt that he and I had become something more than *maître d'* and dinner patron—indeed, I felt that we had become compatriots in cuisine. I actually found myself not hating him much at all!

"Tell me," I said as I paid the check at the table, "does it not bother you sometimes that you operate a restaurant devoted to cannibalism?"

"Ah," he said with a smile, "one must pursue one's passion, and *madame* forgets that this is California, where the improbable happens every day and the impossible not less than once a week." And upon some reflection and a ladylike hiccup, this made perfect sense to me.

The *maître d'* looked around and lowered his voice conspiratorially. "And our costs are surprisingly low," he continued. "Many of our *clientèle* arrive with, for example, their spouse or their employer, yet end up being seated at a table for one, if *madame* takes my meaning."

"I believe I understand you perfectly, sir," I said with an impish smile.

"Would you mind," I said as I was preparing to leave, "if I brought a close friend, a Mr. Earl by name, to L'Homme next week to experience your wonderful cuisine in, shall we say, an intimate fashion?"

"Not at all," said the *maître d'* as I walked toward the door. "Am I to take it that *madame* will once again be dining alone?"

I giggled at this. "'Donner, party of one', my friend," I said. "And I look forward to another delightful meal at L'Homme."

I opened the restaurant's door, ready to dash through the rain to the waiting taxi. "If you should come across a good recipe for cab driver in the meantime I must insist that you share it with me!"

"*Certainement!*"

You Called

Leandra Logan

OCTOBER 28

Paula Hunt had no use for an answering machine. After a long day of clerking at the license bureau, she would simply come home for a look at her telephone's Caller ID. Settling in her recliner with a tumbler of Gallo, she'd hit the review button on her old clumsy cordless to start her evening entertainment.

Four missed calls, she noted tonight with a satisfied slurp of wine.

8:22 a.m.: Helen Morris, Paula's twin sister in Ohio. Paula wasn't about to unearth the long distance phone card given her by Helen. Her widowed sister had, after all, raised four kids on her own, so she should realize how tired Paula must be at this hour. If it was urgent, she'd have to call back.

11:35 a.m.: Care Dentistry. They'd sent her an appointment postcard! She'd call back tomorrow about this useless reminder.

2:27 p.m.: A 1-800 nuisance. Paula jabbed redial. "Hello. You called." Judging by the din, she'd reached a pit of telemarketers. "So what are you selling? Aluminum siding? Why, my home is solid brick. Built in 1923 by my grandfather. In any case, this number is off limits. I'm on every Do Not Call list known to man, that's why! Call twice more and I'll collect a fine. Carpet King did and I'm now the proud owner of a dishwasher with five speeds." She disconnected in a huff.

6:03 p.m.: D. Spooner. The rare random stranger! She gave redial a triumphant tap, only to have the phone ring emptily. She was about to give up when she heard a click. "Hello?"

"Can I help you?" The voice was masculine, smooth as the holiday brandy her parents used to serve here in this room.

A sensual tingle left her momentarily discombobulated.

"Who is this, please?"

She cleared her throat. "You called."

"I don't follow."

"You called me. Not forty minutes ago."

"I did?"

"I arrived home to find the name D. Spooner, and this number on my Caller ID. As I don't recognize—"

"You follow up on calls from strangers who have left no message?"

"Well, yes."

"Why?" The brandy voice held a trace of amusement that made her smile. Charming men seemed an endangered species these days. Those on county business were normally brusque, anxious to get their passport or license renewed. They seldom extended her any courtesy, no matter how she wore her hair.

"I have a right to know who intrudes my space," she replied pertly.

"But if a stranger hasn't left you a message, it's bound to be a misdial."

"Ah, but it's my prerogative to get to the bottom of things."

"Oh, I see, a tenacious lady." He sounded both lamented and pleased.

Paula felt a blush. "I don't suppose...you called me on purpose?"

"Afraid my secretary's sloppy message is to blame. My

apologies…Miss?"

"I am a Miss. Happily single, by the way, D. Spooner."

"So you live alone, Miss Unavailable?"

"Who?"

"On my ID screen you're coming up as Unavailable."

"Ah."

"It's not much to go on."

"A lady can't be too careful these days, even a tenacious one."

"Makes it tough to get friendly, find out how unavailable you really are."

"As it happens, I do live alone—happily alone."

"Hmm."

"What do you mean?"

"Forgive me for saying so, but you sound a bit lonely."

"I'm alone by choice! Because I choose to be."

"Let's be clear," he drawled. "No boyfriend will clean my clock if I happen to call you on purpose next time?"

Paula bubbled with glee. "You'd be safe."

"I only ask because I'm lonely myself. And you're so easy to talk to."

"Right back at you, D. Spooner."

"The D stands for David," he ventured.

"This has been really fun. David."

"Can you hang on a sec?" She heard a clatter, then moments later he was back. "Sorry about that," he said. "I am serious about calling again."

"Oh. I don't know…It's against my policy to leap into anything."

"Are you deep into policies?"

"Entrenched in civil service," she chirped, "structure and protocol, correct forms and proper channels."

"Public service is always something to be proud of."

"Public service. How nice."

"I'm in public service myself."

"Really. What branch?"

"A tale for another time. Say, you could call me till we're better acquainted."

"You win, David. Same time, same place then?"

"I'm rarely here after hours. Suppose I can trust you with my cell number. Got a pen?"

OCTOBER 29

"I wasn't going to call you, David."

"Why not?"

"Oh, it all seems so adolescent."

"What's the matter with feeling young?"

She giggled. "Nothing, I suppose."

"So, how was your day?"

Paula railed on about license applicants. The woman who undercut her weight, the man who wore makeup for his photo. "It's official business, not Glamour Shots! People should face reality. Always better to be genuine."

"Very wise," he agreed sagely. The conversation faltered briefly. Then sweetly, she thought, he asked what she had for lunch.

"An apple."

"That's all?"

"I used the time to buy some blackout shades for my front room. I intend to get them up tonight."

"Are you being bothered?"

"Oh, no. Normally I sit in dark on Halloween to discourage trick-or-treaters. This way I can turn on a lamp or two."

"Not interested in giving out candy?"

"I kept up the tradition after my parents died. Then I missed a year with a sprained ankle and decided to stop altogether."

He sighed. "Children can be annoying."

"I enjoy the small goblins. But it's against my principles to give treats to anyone over eleven. I'm forced to decipher ages on the spot, causing a stressful bottleneck on the front walk. The high traffic is our family's own fault, I suppose, for giving out the freshest Tootsie Rolls."

"Nothing better!"

"One Halloween, we ran out." She merrily launched into the details. "Goodnight, David," she said much later. "Thanks for listening. It's a dying art."

"I feel rather silly, trying to romance a girl who won't share her name."

Romance. He said it flat out! Could it happen this fast? She'd seen *Last Chance Harvey* and it had been like that for Harvey and Kate.

"Well, eat a better lunch tomorrow—"

"Paula," she erupted. "I'm named after the tune, Hey, Paula." She sang a few bars and soon they were harmonizing. "Not just anybody would know the lyrics to that old love song," she whispered.

"I'm not just anybody. Goodnight. Paula."

OCTOBER 30

"My senior prom was a disaster!" Paula was sloshed fifteen minutes into this talk with David. It was, after all, a Friday night and she always imbibed more on Fridays. As much as she hated the desolate Saturday to follow, she celebrated the fact that she didn't have to face her dull job for two days. "Robby Page showed interest, but couldn't afford the cost. I thought to invite him here instead. Dad moved the dining room table so we could dance, like they'd be doing at the Crystal Ballroom. Mom bought some records to replace the band. Oops, I sound old."

"No worries. I had an album collection myself."

"Figured I could drift off in his arms and be at prom in every way that mattered."

"What happened, Paula?"

She jammed a tissue under her runny nose. "Rich bitch Bonny Ray paid his way at the last minute. Nobody told me! I waited and waited, dressed in a green taffeta gown and matching pumps, both a size too small. If only he'd called. The shoes were killing me by ten o'clock."

"That's low. I hope he had a miserable time."

"My sister couldn't wait to report that he was a great dancer. Guess there's some good in everyone," she sniffled half-heartedly.

"I got turned down myself, junior and senior year."

"No way."

"My older brother had all the pizzazz. Still does."

"That's how it is with me and Helen! We're identical twins, yet everyone gravitates toward *her*. Naturally she landed a husband fast—before we finished secretarial school. She's been widowed for years, but it hasn't stopped her lucky streak. She's living it up in Ohio with devoted children."

"Hey, Paula, I have an idea. Why don't I come by on Halloween? We can wear costumes, do a little dancing in the dining room."

"I was planning a quiet night."

"For no reason at all."

"Okay. If you bring the Tootsie Rolls."

"No worries. If you'll please tell me where you live!"

OCTOBER 31

David was late. Worse, he wasn't answering his cell. Paula prowled her kitchen in a strapless black taffeta dress, a velour mask across her eyes—an edgy cat fueled by raw nerves and a bellyful of Chablis.

She'd been stood up on occasion since Robby. The co-worker who flirted at the Christmas party, then sobered up only to forget. The salesman who'd sold her cookware with the bogus promise of returning for dinner.

Had David changed his mind as well? Maybe it had all been in the chase.

Would calling his landline appear desperate? She could claim to need wine. It wouldn't be too hard to conceal her stockpile of Gallo in the basement. Well, wearing this dress and an alcohol buzz, it would be a challenge. She'd call first to see if she needed an excuse. He might even be flattered by her concern.

Moving through the house, cozily aglow this Halloween behind her blackout shades, she lowered the volume of the old hi-fi in the dining room, then walked to the front room. Picking up her cordless, she removed the block on her own identity. After all, she was now anxious to reveal herself to him totally. She scrolled the Caller ID list for D. Spooner and hit redial.

A woman answered. Jealousy bit, but only briefly. This was, after all, his business line. "I'd like to speak to Mr. Spooner," she said crisply.

"Mr. Spooner?"

"Yes. David Spooner."

"You have the wrong number."

"Huh! I never do. I went to secretarial school."

"I'm afraid I don't understand..."

It was late. Likely the muttering woman was on the cleaning crew. "Let me speak to your supervisor," Paula requested.

There was a pause, yet the same voice returned. "Paula Hunt, is it?"

Hearing her name thrown back at her after years of caller anonymity was disconcerting. "Yes."

"You sound too mature for a Halloween prank."

"I beg your pardon. This conversation is no joke—for my part anyway."

"Why, I resent your implication. You called me, remember?"

So she had. Suddenly Paula was on the receiving end of her own tactics. "Look," she shrilled, "I demand you put D. Spooner on the line!"

"There is nothing I'd like better to do."

"So you do know David."

"No. D. Spooner was my daughter. Denise. She used an initial for safety reasons. For all the good it did her."

"What?"

"Denise was strangled. Here in her home on the twenty-eighth." The women's voice broke on the last few words.

"But I called this number that very night. I spoke to a David."

"Ms. Hunt, you likely spoke to her murderer!"

"You're wrong. My David's delightful, charming!"

"That's the Dreamboat's MO." The woman sounded upset. "The serial killer the police suspect."

"There must be a mistake."

"The Dreamboat is a pro. He worms his way into a woman's life, often via the Internet, then moves in for the kill. It's vital you talk to the police—before he tracks you down. Hello? Hello?"

Paula was distracted by a silhouette in the kitchen doorway. A dashing tuxedo-clad figure wearing a rubber mask of Fred Astaire, balancing a sack of Tootsie Rolls.

"Hey, hey, Paula," he sang out. "Sorry to be late. Stopped for the candy. Who's that on the telephone?"

"Only Helen, David," she lilted uncertainly.

"Thought I heard my name as I came through the back door."

Which she kept locked. Had she forgotten? "I was telling her about us. I'm sure she's jealous."

He sauntered over to listen in. "She's gone. Do your schtick, hit redial."

"Forget her. Tonight is ours."

Surely any serial killer worth his salt would commandeer her best link to the outside. He calmly returned hers to its charger. "The music calls." He tossed aside the candy and jauntily extended his arm. "Lead on."

She froze mid-smile. By all appearances, this was the sensitive man with whom she shared so much in common, a true kindred spirit. To throw it away on the word of a strange female with unknown motives was something she couldn't bring herself to do.

They moved to the dining room, romance central with playing hi-fi, flickering sconces, dinette set pushed to one side. Gently he swept her up and expertly cut across the floor. She closed her eyes, denial and dreams swirling round her tipsy head. Other couples were happy, applying for marriage licenses all the time. It had to be her turn.

The doorbell rang on occasion and muted shouts of 'trick-or-treat!' penetrated the house's ancient windows. Shut away behind the blackout shades, they danced on without interruption. David performed superbly, poised and limber, twirling her round, lifting her off the floor with impressive strength.

The music slowed, by her preconceived design. David rocked her in a lazy sway. "Tell me, Paula, who was that really on the phone?"

"I told you."

He sighed. "You called the other number, didn't you?"

"Oh, David!" she lamented. "I was just so eager to see you."

"Naturally."

"Was it some crazed associate I spoke to?"

"Do you want it to be?"

"I want the truth."

His eyes glittered behind the mask. "No woman ever has yet."

"Oh, please…"

"Please what, Paula? Be the man of your dreams?"

"Yes," she whimpered, quaking against his chest.

"No worries." He twirled her off again. At music's end, they rested before the mirrored buffet. Her round raccoon-masked face and his rubbery caricature of Fred Astaire loomed bizarrely amidst the reflection of china and crystal.

Slipping back, he began to skillfully massage her bare shoulders. She luxuriated against his lean solid form. One hand soon escaped down the slippery fabric of her tight dress and palmed her belly, pushing her tush deep into his solid erection. They shared a pleasured moan.

"I can make you happy, David."

"You already are."

"We might even fall in love."

"Afraid not, old girl."

She shivered warily. "Because of that awful woman on the phone."

"Not because of her."

"Why then?"

"Sadly, I am incapable of loving anyone. And your love life," he added above her gasp, "is already too crowded."

"I…don't understand."

"Shh… No worries…" The hand on her belly roved lower, dipping under her hemline to skim her plump inner thigh.

Her squeal of surprise dissolved to an agonized whimper as he cruelly twisted her tender flesh.

Panting in her ear, he invaded the edge of her panties. "You've had your fun in the driver's seat. It's my turn to steer."

Her heart pounding in realization, a terrified Paula blinked back tears. This gamble of a lifetime would likely cost her her life.

Time stretched on torturously, braced against the Dreamboat, caught in his cruel grip. Trembling in revulsion over his escalating liberties, her imminent demise, Paula began to simmer over a lifetime of disappointments. Until with wild guttural sounds she tore free, viciously clawing off his rubber face—and a handful of hair in the bargain!

She staggered back on a fresh wave of nausea. She'd been conned not by a pedigreed rogue of middle age, but a slimy young earthworm with a polished head and slash of brow! A man without a single attractive feature. "Impossible," she breathed.

He giggled eerily. "Mimicry and mirrors, is all. I just fed you back your own delusions." When she continued to gape, he shoved her in the direction of the buffet, then yanked down her mask. "Have another look. There's your one true love."

She stared at her bare, weather-beaten face reflected in the glass, so unlike the poised image she carried of herself.

"My own self-righteous gram was my first venture into public service. Locked me in her closet once too often. Had to strangle her with one of Granddad's ties. No worries, though. Gave her a cup of tea and sang her a song. I'm still trying to match the thrill, over and over. Denise came close. All because of you."

With a flourish, he tightened Paula's mask round her throat. "You called. And I can't thank you enough. Denise got away to answer the ringing phone. I couldn't risk hanging up and raising an alarm. Killing her while we talked was one sweet rush. Lining up my next biddy, a bonus!"

Desperately Paula clawed at the velour cinch crushing her air passage. He'd actually murdered Denise Spooner while they bandied words. Maybe she deserved to drown in horror and disgrace, with her dress bunched at her waist.

Suddenly the cinch slacked.

"Say, why don't we spice this up with a call to Helen? I could pop in on her next, regift those Tootsies." Hauling Paula to the living room, he snagged the cordless and held it out. "Dial. I'll do the rest."

"Not Helen," she seethed. "Not ever."

Clapping a hand on her mouth, he cracked her on the side of the head with the phone. "This thing's like a club," he marveled as she wobbled, hair matted in blood.

She was fading fast, losing her footing. Then the doorbell rang. It was just enough of a distraction. She seized the phone and hurled it at the only window without a blackout shade, a stained glass one. Before losing consciousness she was satisfied to hear breaking glass.

Paula awoke in a hospital bed to find Helen at her side.

"You can rest easy. They got him with a bullet between the eyes."

Paula sagged against her pillows.

"You and that Caller ID! This all started because Denise Spooner phoned to solicit a donation to the Heart Fund. The cops dug deeper and found your name on a call list."

"One mystery solved."

"But not the mystery of how you, a sensible woman—"

"Had a dream? Don't look so smug, fancy pants. He was coming after you next!"

Helen had the grace to cringe. "They do say he was a master at role play. He'd become Mr. Perfect then move in for the kill. Apparently Denise fancied a biker toy boy, hence his shaved head."

"Wonder how many died."

"Lots. You got off lucky."

"Yes. Lucky I was able to throw the phone, lucky it was a night the neighbors were out to see it. I must thank them in some way."

Helen hesitated. "It was Denise's mother who called the cops. Nobody else."

"Nobody?"

"The house was black, remember? You've sent a clear message that you don't want to be disturbed."

"I screamed and broke a window!"

"Both easily dismissed on Halloween."

"But we're an original family on the street. Popular!"

"Things change. Many families have moved away."

"Some of the other houses have been passed through the generations. Those people know me."

"But they don't like you anymore, Paula. Your high-handedness turns them off."

"High *standards*. Nothing wrong with having those."

"You've become too isolated, set in your ways. It's gotten so bad you're pouncing on wrong numbers for company!"

"Guess I'm lonelier than I realized," she finally begrudged.

"Like it or not, this creature found you ripe for the picking."

Paula blushed. "I should have realized something was wrong when he agreed with everything I said."

"Yes, you should. A prince like that is either straight out of Cinderella or—"

"Or the wolf out of Little Red Riding Hood," Paula finished.

As they shared a laugh Helen handed her a gift. "From the kids."

"No card?"

"No need. Their Aunt Paula is smart enough to get the message."

Paula tore off the paper. To find an answering machine.

The Ogre of Her Dreams

Marilyn Victor

"Your homework over the Samhain break is to undo the spell I've just conjured upon you." Olympia Dalrymple inhaled her students' horror with malevolent pleasure. With few exceptions, the fledgling witches were totally clueless. While she conjured up the simplest of spells, they had fidgeted and pretended to listen to her lecture on the rare Narcissine tree frog. She could have told them the frogs were the trapped souls of lackluster students and they wouldn't have paid attention. She'd give a fistful of faeries to wipe those simpering smiles from the little demons' faces.

Well, they weren't all demons—Hell's children had only recently been admitted to the Dalrymple School of the Arts. But from her perspective, standing at the head of the class, they may as well have been. One wave of her hand and they'd all be gone. Permanently.

With difficulty, she composed her thoughts onto a more benign track. If any of them had had the ambition to move ahead in their textbooks—which she very much doubted—they might very well be reading her mind. Better to keep all unkind thoughts to herself. She'd already spent a couple of Samhains deep in Hell's kitchen and had no desire to repeat the experience.

A young witch in the front row began to whine. "You told us that a spell couldn't be undone."

Olympia's lips turned up into a mirthless smile. "I did, didn't I?"

"But how—"

"If you had paid attention instead of passing notes you might have the answer." She waved her hand toward the door. "Now off with you and enjoy your holiday." *And may a troll bite off your heads before you return to my class.* Retirement was looking better and better all the time. Only twenty-five more years and she'd be out of here.

❖

Olympia gently placed the struggling frog back in its terrarium. It immediately hopped into the corner, blinking baby blue eyes at her. She stooped down and stared into the humid glass container she'd designed especially for her collection. Only one left. She was either going to have to cut back on her spelling or get some more frogs. Either option could be problematic.

"Mrs. D."

What now? She turned stiffly toward the voice. Miss Piddleworth. Of course. Who else would dare bother her after being dismissed?

Aurora Piddleworth stood with her back against the closed classroom door. She was still wearing the costume from this afternoon's pre-Samhain celebration. In Olympia's day Samhain costumes were all about being as scary and loathsome as possible, all the better to scare an evil spirit or demon back to the Etherworld. Today, human influence was more prevalent and young Miss Piddleworth had dressed her developing young figure in an all-too-revealing cheerleader's outfit. One no human mother would allow her daughter out the door wearing.

Aurora was staring at her, full red lips turned up in a smile which said she was already congratulating herself on her cleverness. Olympia was certain she wouldn't have to wait long to discover exactly what Miss Piddleworth based this assumption of cleverness on. Patience was not the girl's virtue.

Aurora sauntered further into the small classroom, trailing a finger across the desk and having the gall to plop herself into her teacher's chair. With studied coyness, she dipped down and pulled a small, worn book from her *Twilight* backpack.

"Where did you get that, girl?" Olympia asked, giving her voice just the right amount of indignation and anger so as to give the young girl a moment's pause. But only a moment's.

"I found it in the library." Aurora's voice sing-songed, dragging out the word library as if daring her teacher to disagree with her.

Olympia tried to snatch the book from her, but Aurora Piddleworth held it just out of reach, blond curls bouncing about her flat round face.

"That is a forbidden text, Ms. Piddleworth. If the head mistress hears about this—"

"But she won't, will she? Because it came from your *secret library.*"

Olympia arched an eyebrow at the young girl.

"You've taught us well, Mrs. D. It was amazingly easy." She slanted her golden eyes up at her teacher. "I always suspected there was a bit of the vagrant beneath that icy exterior of yours."

"What do you want?" Olympia was not about to indulge the girl in condescending chitchat.

"A soulmate." Aurora mouthed the word as if it was some secret aphrodisiac.

Olympia rolled her eyes. Obviously, the nitwit teaching Potions 101 was using Shakespeare as an example again. Instead of a cautionary tale for the misuse of sleeping potions, the story of Romeo and Juliet simply fired up already raging hormones.

Aurora tossed the book on the table, causing Olympia to wince. It was an old book. And a very rare one.

Aurora flipped carelessly through the pages. "It says here that every witch has a soulmate. Why weren't we told about this?" She looked up imploringly with those golden eyes, more like a hungry cat than a young witch.

"Be careful what you wish for," Olympia warned.

"Oh, *pleeeazee*. I know your history. It's no secret. I want a soulmate just as much as you ever did, maybe more."

"You're too young."

"I'm over one hundred years," the girl huffed. At her teacher's hard stare she acquiesced. "Well, I will be after graduating."

"Much too young to be thinking of such things." Olympia turned her back on the young witch, inwardly smiling at the girl's foolishness.

Aurora toppled her chair and stood next to the teacher, fists clenched. "I. Want. One."

Olympia could feel the energy rolling across her like a thundercloud. Aurora was powerful. There was no denying that. She came from a very old and formidable bloodline.

"Sit. Down." Olympia ordered. "Before you burn something up."

Aurora dropped down in the chair again, her full lips set in a petulant pout. "If you don't do as I say, I'll tell Headmistress and you'll be tossed out. No severance. No retirement. My mother said so."

The headmistress might be Olympia's sister, but she wouldn't think twice about expelling her older sibling. "You seem to have given this some thought."

"Oh, I have." The young witch's voice was childish again, and she began flipping through the book. "Some of the pages are missing, but I've read most of it. Samhain is only a couple of days away, and it says here it can only happen on that evening if there's a full moon—and there will be one. I checked."

"Not Sam-Haine, Sah-win," Olympia automatically corrected.

"Whatever. All we have to do—"

"We?"

Aurora gave her a peeved look. "It says here," she jammed her finger at a passage on the faded pages, "that a level four witch has to perform the bonding ceremony."

"Your mother's a level four, have her do it."

"Are you crazy?" Her golden eyes were wide with horror. "If my mother knew what I was up to, she'd turn me to stone and send me to the second dimension until I agreed to marry that horrible Manger boy."

Olympia knew the Manger boy and felt an iota of sympathy for the girl, still she felt compelled to support tradition. "Mothers usually know what's best for their daughters."

"But you have experience. You conjured up a soulmate for yourself when you were my age. Now I want you to do the same for me." When Olympia made no sign of caving in, Aurora glared at her, slammed the book shut and stood up. "I believe the headmistress is still in her office, is she not?"

Olympia folded her arms across her chest, remaining silent.

Aurora walked toward the door, looking over her shoulder. "Goodbye retirement, hello banishment."

She had her hand on the doorknob when Olympia stopped her. "Meet me at my house an hour before midnight on Samhain Eve. And come alone. There must be no distractions." Or witnesses.

❖

Aurora had never been on time for anything in her life. Tonight was different. Tonight she was going to meet the man of her dreams. Her soulmate. A man she could make real magic with. She already knew exactly what he would look like. He'd be tall, with dark curly hair and maybe he'd wear glasses. Glasses could be so sexy on a gorgeous man. Like Clark Kent.

The street in front of Miss Dalrymple's house was deserted, all the mundanes in their pathetic Halloween costumes having retreated to their homes to drool over their loot. She wished them all excruciating abdominal distress and blackened teeth for their lack of self-control.

She used the oversized doorknocker to announce her arrival.

Talk about Addams Family. The house looked every bit of its two hundred years. It needed paint. Hell, it needed a complete facelift. Obviously, Mrs. D.'s husband wasn't too handy around the house. But who needed handy when you had true love.

It hadn't taken her long to learn the truth about her teacher. How Mrs. D. had defied her parents and the witches council and conjured up a spell that attracted her soulmate. Then she had run away with him, spurning her family for true love. If Mrs. D. could do it, so could Aurora. She just had to find Mr. Right. And tonight was the night.

The door creaked open and Mrs. Dalrymple stood in the pale light. She was still a beautiful woman, Aurora would give her that. By human standards she barely looked a day over forty. She would have looked even younger if it weren't for that pinched-face superior expression she always wore.

Mrs. D. led her through the quiet halls of the house and down into the basement. It was damp and musty smelling. Jars lined the shelves of her workroom, filled with all the things they had discussed in class and some that they hadn't. Bats wings. Newts eyes. Dragon hair. An aquarium of crickets sang in the corner, next to a terrarium with that blue-eyed frog Mrs. D. had brought to class the other day.

On the corner of the workbench sat a framed photo of one of the most beautiful men she had ever imagined—and she could imagine quite a bit.

"My husband. Jeffrey," Mrs. D. explained as if reading her thoughts.

So the rumors were true. A quiver of excitement went through her. How could Mrs. D. be so freakin' uptight when she had a gorgeous hunk like that to come home to every night?

"Are you sure this is what you want?" her teacher asked again as she lit white candles around the room, illuminating the dark corners.

"YES." She almost stamped her foot in frustration. "How many times are you going to ask me that?"

"Three more. It's part of the ritual."

Aurora swallowed down her irritation. She supposed it was a little enough price to pay for a lifetime of bliss. Each time Mrs. D. posed her questions, she answered in the affirmative. When she answered the last one she asked, "Now what?"

Mrs. D. smiled and lifted the struggling frog from its terrarium. Aurora wrinkled her nose in disgust. She hated frogs. They were cold and slimy, and this one winked terrified blue eyes at her as Mrs. Dalrymple wielded a sharp knife in front of its amphibian nose.

"Now hold still, darling," Olympia cooed to the frog. "We just want a bit of blood. There's a good girl."

Like a doctor with a scalpel, she drew a small incision along the frog's throat, droplets of bright red blood oozing instantly from the wound. She held a small granite spell cup beneath it, counting each drop as it fell.

"Wouldn't it be easier to just kill the stupid thing?" Aurora asked, impatient for the ceremony to begin. She wasn't getting any younger.

Mrs. D. glared at her. "Life is precious. No matter how short that life is."

"It's just a frog."

"This particular frog is very hard to come by." Mrs. D. dipped a swab of some foul-smelling stuff across the wound, and it instantly sealed itself. Aurora's eyes widened. It took immense power to perform a healing, even on a frog.

Other ingredients were added to the cup until a ghostly vapor began to rise and twirl above it. A dank, putrid smell swirled into the room, as if someone had just upped the contents of their stomach on the floor.

Mrs. D. thrust the cup at her. "Drink."

Aurora recoiled, stumbling back until she leaned against the terrarium. Mrs. D.'s eyes were now totally black, the strength of the spell she was spinning already pulling her deep into its magic. Swallowing hard, Aurora reached for the cup, and, trying not to think about it, drank the evil mixture as quickly as she could.

Mrs. D.'s smile portended no good will. "What is done cannot be undone."

Like she'd want to. Aurora wiped a trickle of the potion from her chin. With all their power and magic, why was it that all potions tasted like the bottom of a swamp?

"Now what?" she asked, shivering with a sudden chill.

"We wait."

In a corner cage, a small bat stretched its wings. The crickets went silent. Two heartbeats later, a heavy knock fell upon the upstairs door, as if delivered with a cudgel rather than a fist.

Aurora's eyes widened. "Ohhh. He's strong," she cooed, knowing in her heart that her one true love had arrived. Glad that she had brought along a soda to wash away the wicked taste that still lingered in her mouth, she raced up the stone stairway.

Without waiting for Mrs. D., she threw the door open, stumbling back with a gasp. The man—no, the Thing—standing in front of her was the Hunchback of Notre Dame. He was no taller than her shoulder, and just as wide. His rheumy eyes looked into her golden ones with amusement.

"I've been waiting for you all my life," he told her, shuffling across the threshold on short legs, his knuckles trailing across the floor as he moved forward. "What took you so long, babe?"

Aurora spun around and grabbed hold of her teacher. "What have you done? This isn't what I signed up for."

Mrs. D.'s smile was unsympathetic. "I warned you."

An inhuman laugh bellowed behind her, and a heavy hand lowered on her shoulder. Aurora stiffened, turned slowly around, and almost fainted.

Standing in front of her was the singularly best looking young man she had ever set eyes on. He looked like a blond George Clooney, only his eyelashes were longer and darker.

He waggled his eyebrows at her. "Had you going, didn't I?"

"What...a...eh...."

"Well, it is Halloween isn't it? Trick-or-treat?" He grinned, his smile filled with perfect white teeth. "I thought I'd go for the trick."

"You're drooling, darling," Mrs. D. admonished, giving her student a pointed look.

Aurora wiped her mouth, never taking her amber gold eyes off her soulmate. He wasn't only drop-dead gorgeous, he was smart and powerful. Not many witches would have been able to hold a disguise spell like that.

He gently took her hand and raised it to his lips. He was obviously under her spell, too. He couldn't take his eyes off of her. Wait until she told her friends. They were going to be so jealous.

❖

If Olympia Dalrymple had been a gambler, she would have given Aurora Piddleworth two weeks, three at most. To her surprise, it was nearly a month before the girl stormed into her empty classroom, slamming the door behind her.

"You've got to get rid of him!" she demanded, gasping for breath as if she'd been running all morning.

She no longer looked like the young ingénue she'd been when she'd first walked into Mrs. Dalrymple's classroom. There was no bravado, no self-centered smile on the young face now. In fact, she looked quite desperate and disheveled.

"Once a spell is in place it cannot be undone. It was in Lesson 101, had you been paying attention." At the chalkboard, Olympia began writing out the next day's lessons.

"You can do another spell. Poison him. Turn him into a frog! I don't care. Just. Get. Rid. Of him!"

Olympia turned, a superior smile lighting up her face. "Do I detect some trouble in paradise? Is your soulmate not all you thought he'd be?"

"He's an ogre!"

"Of course he is, my dear. That's what a witch's soulmate is.

Didn't you read the book?"

Aurora threw the object of discussion on the table. "Take it! I don't want it!"

"It's right there on page ..." Olympia lifted the ancient tome with an exaggerated gesture and leafed slowly through the brown pages. She looked up in mock consternation. "That page seems to be missing." Her smile was not friendly. "But not to worry. This spell only has a shelf life of five hundred years. After that, you'll be free of him."

"Aurora!" The high-pitched whining voice of an ogre called to her from somewhere in the school's halls.

Aurora turned wild eyes on her teacher. "Five-hundred years! I can't possibly wait five hundred years! I'll be an old woman! You have to do something."

"You have a great power, my dear. But it wasn't given to you to be squandered on selfish impulses. There are consequences. Magic does not exist to feed our every whim. Once it is brought into the world, it cannot be destroyed."

Shaking, Aurora looked back at the door with terror-filled eyes. "He's horrible. He's ugly. He smells bad. He—"

"—loves you," Olympia finished for her. "That's what you wanted, isn't it?"

"Oh, Aurora!" The ogre called again to his soulmate. He was getting closer.

Aurora grabbed hold of Olympia's shirt. "Please, you have to help me. I'll do anything."

"Anything?"

The young girl nodded vigorously. "Hurry. Please. Before he finds me again. I can't stand to look at him anymore."

"Well, there is one thing I could do." Olympia was silent for a moment, pretending to give Aurora's dilemma some thought. "I have a spell that would allow me to hide you from him. Would that be acceptable?"

This time Olympia didn't bother to conceal her smile at the terrified young witch's ready agreement.

❖

"It won't be long now, Jeffrey," Olympia promised, smiling at the gargantuan ogre that guiltily removed his finger from his nose when she addressed him.

She glanced at the photo sitting on her workbench, reminding her of why she went to the lengths she did.

Olympia set her spell cup next to the terrarium. This time she would brew up a double-strength potion. This frog's blood should keep Jeffrey in his more appealing form through the next Samhain at least. Maybe longer. She allowed a sigh to escape. Twenty-five more years and her sentence would be over. She'd be free of him and she could retire.

She slid the cover off the terrarium. There were two frogs cowering in the corner now. She reached in and scooped up the newest addition to her collection. The yellow one with the golden eyes.

She laughed as it struggled to get away. "You should have listened to me, dear," she soothed, as she raised the scalpel to its throat. But they never did.

Motherly Intuition

Julia Buckley

Daphne's mother died on the first of September, and Daphne found that her grief was deeper and more painful than she could have anticipated. But who can anticipate the feeling of loss, especially the loss of a mother?

When she started hearing the voices, she thought perhaps the stress and grief had made her insane. There were conversations happening in her head, complicated back-and-forths which suggested schizophrenia. Daphne, always pragmatic, went to a therapist.

"I'm thirty-four and I'm hearing a voice in my head."

"Is there a history of mental illness in your family?" asked the psychiatrist, a gray-headed woman with a grandmotherly aura.

"No. I mean, my mother and I always accused each other of being insane, but we weren't actually."

The voice in her head started laughing.

"See—it's happening now. Someone's laughing in there."

"What do you mean, you called each other insane?"

"Oh—uh. You'd have to understand our dynamic. We insulted each other out of love, sometimes."

"In what way?"

"I mean, like, I'd tell her that her cooking sucked, which it did. But I'd say it was terrible and we'd both laugh, and she'd say that I sucked as a daughter, and then we'd eat her bad dinner and it diffused all the tension that you get when you lie to people."

You suck as a patient, too. She thinks you're truly insane.

"Be quiet," Daphne said.

The therapist frowned and took out a prescription pad.

But two weeks into taking Prozac, Daphne didn't feel better, and the voice didn't go away. The voice insisted that Daphne should know it, recognize it. *Daphne. I'm your mother*, it told her.

"Like hell you are. My mother would have the decency to leave me alone."

I'm here for a reason.

"Yeah? What?"

I don't know yet. It's kind of hard to figure out this new world, okay? Cut me some slack. I just know that I need to protect my daughter.

"Maybe I'm just insane, and this is an offshoot of my grief. Maybe I just want you to be there."

Do you? That's so sweet.

"I miss my mom. And I'm not convinced you're her."

Why?

"You're less annoying."

That's because I'm not physically present.

"True."

But I still love you, and that's what matters.

"You know, I can't go along with this until you prove it. Prove you're not just my brain being weird. Tell me a secret that only my mother knows. Something I can verify."

Okay. Let's see here. I've got it. I used to read lots of erotica. Especially after I turned forty. But I didn't want you or your brother to ever find it because it contained words like "fuck" and "cum." Other words, too, funny words, looking back. So I hid it in my bedroom. You know where the fuse box is? When you open that door, there's a little area off to the side. Almost like a little shelf, and a bag with books inside. My stash.

"Erotica is a euphemism, you know."

Just check the fuse box at my house; your brother just about has it ready to put on the market.

Daphne did, and there they were. Books called things like *Angry Highland Rebel* and *Love's Yearning Thrust.*

"Yuck," Daphne said.

Judge not, said the voice. *And I'd rather have my stash of euphemisms than your last three boyfriends.*

"Touché, Mom."

❖

They settled into a routine over the next few weeks. Her mother promised to appear only when Daphne had a quiet moment. She wouldn't bother her at the bookstore, where Daphne was usually far too busy cashiering or shelving to manage an extra voice, and she wouldn't appear when Daphne went on dates.

There were many advantages, they agreed, to being together only in spirit. There weren't those uncomfortable problems of eye contact—too much? Too little? Nor were there questions later about what someone's words or expressions *really* meant— the sort of things that bruised the hearts of family members, even made them stop speaking to each other.

In the case of two minds blending, there was never an ambiguous moment.

One day, when Daphne got home from work and put up her feet for the first time that day, she closed her eyes. "Mom?"

Yes?

Did it hurt? Dying?

Quiet laughter. *The funny thing is, the worst part about dying is the years we spend dreading it. Remember that line in* Julius Caesar? *A coward dies many times before his death . . . .*

So it's not so bad?

No. Except the leaving. But then I found a way . . . .

Can you talk to Jason?

No. I don't know why. I would ask you to give him a message, but you know Jason. He'd send you back to the psychiatrist.

Daphne laughed. "Yes, he would."

Daphne.

"Yes?"

There's something I have to prevent. Something with a man.

"Oh, please. You're going to give a thumbs down to every guy I date?"

No, this isn't about dating. I want you to find a nice man, to enjoy him.

"Like in 'Love's Yearning Thrust?'"

Among other things.

"So what's to prevent?"

I don't know. But I'll be here. I guess that's what this is all about.

"But that means that there's such a thing as fate, right?"

No. Because if it were fate, I couldn't change it.

❖

The next day Daphne spent a long time in the storeroom unpacking boxes. Karl, from shipping and receiving, stood over her with his giant tape roll, chatting about a movie he'd seen. He gave just about every plot secret away.

"Karl, have you ever heard of a spoiler warning?" she asked testily, knifing open another box.

"Sorry," he said, reddening. "I assumed you didn't want to see it. You said you didn't like scary movies."

"I don't. When did I say that?"

"That time I asked if you wanted to go see *Paranormal Activity* with me."

"Oh." She looked up at him then. "Well why didn't you ever ask me to see something else?"

"I don't know. I figured that was just an excuse."

"It wasn't. I was telling the truth. But you shouldn't tell people the endings of movies unless they ask you to."

He shrugged. "Good to know, Daphne." He went back to his work area, peeved for some reason.

Men, Daphne thought.

Toward lunch an irate customer came to the counter. He was an older man, tall and portly. "Your science fiction section is woefully inadequate. You only have one Stephen R. Donaldson on the shelf."

"We normally have more. Perhaps another fan came in earlier. We'll have more soon."

"But he should always be on your shelves, with multiple copies!"

"Not everyone shares your taste. We put out what our distributor sends us. You could always try another store."

"I don't like your attitude. What is your name?" the man said. A classic angry customer gambit. Try to humiliate the cashier by treating her as a menial.

"It's here on my name tag."

"Fine, Daphne Bright. I'll be contacting your supervisors."

"Okay. I'll keep working until they come to get me." She gestured to the line behind him.

He stomped out with one final glare at her. Daphne was used to this. Some people came into the store simply because they *wanted* to yell at someone. That probably hadn't been about Stephen R. Donaldson at all.

She continued waiting on the line, which seemed endless, and didn't get her lunch until two o'clock. She tried to read, but felt too agitated from the day's confrontations to concentrate on the text of the latest thriller.

By five she was more than ready to leave. She strolled into the outdoor mall, a suburban Chicago paradise, and passed the posh shops, the luxury clothiers, the expensive restaurants. Next to Marcel's, under a small elm tree, stood a man smoking a cigarette. "Hey, Daphne," he said.

She peered at him, surprised. He dropped his cigarette, toed it, and came closer.

"It's me," he said. "John Baynor."

"Oh, Mr. Baynor! How are you?"

Daphne hadn't seen this friend of her parents since she was a teen. He'd lived on their block at the time, a chef in some downtown eatery.

Now he pointed at Marcel's. "I work here. Taking a quick cigarette break—a terrible vice for a chef, but I have so few vices left."

He smiled, and she saw that he was attractive still. He'd been younger than her parents—was probably about fifty now. "How's your wife?"

"Married to someone else."

"Oh—sorry."

"Water under the bridge. The kids are happily married, and I'm a single man about town. You work here?"

"Yeah—at Brady's Books."

"Ah. Nice place."

"It is nice. One of the last big bookstores in town."

"The demise of literature on paper."

"I hope not."

"It was great to see you, Daphne. You haven't changed—you still look like a kid. Anyway, I've got to get back to my sauces."

She laughed. "Someday I'll come and have lunch."

"I'll be expecting you. On the house, of course."

Daphne thanked him and waved. Her bad feeling about the day was forgotten.

❖

Men react extremely to you, her mother said that night as Daphne made her dinner.

"What does that mean?"

You either seem to attract them or infuriate them. And even the fury is probably rooted in attraction. Men aren't that complicated, but they don't always understand their own feelings.

"You're a male basher."

No. You had perfectly nice males in your family. Your dad, your brother. But the other men in the world I can't speak for. I just feel the intensity of what they feel.

"Well, let me know if one feels genuine love. I'm a romantic."

❖

For the rest of that week Daphne was busy with work; in the evenings she wanted nothing more than to veg in front of the television.

This is why you don't meet men.

"Where should I go to meet one? A bar?"

I'm saying that you isolate yourself. Join a book group or do some service for the church.

"Why? Is there a God?"

I'm dead and I'm talking to you. Doesn't that make you believe in something?

"Yes. Mom—I'm really glad to have you here."

I know.

"I'll go to church on Sunday. I do go sometimes, you know. Just not all the time."

It's not so much the going as the believing. I have to leave now, Daphne—I'm storing energy.

"For what?"

I don't know. A storm.

"That sounds ominous." But her mother was gone.

❖

There was a storm on Halloween; it hurled itself against the windowpanes of Brady's Books, and yet customers made their way inside.

"This is weird," said Daphne to Karl as he sealed up a package of returns.

"What?"

"The tempest. Someone told me a storm was coming yesterday."

Karl's lip curled. "Tom Skilling, maybe? Weathermen will do that."

"No—no. Never mind."

"Do you feel okay?"

"I feel out of sorts."

"Is that an expression?"

"Yes."

"And it means?"

"I feel weird. Like I shouldn't have gotten out of bed today."

"Are you superstitious?"

"Lately, yes. Not superstitious, exactly, but something."

"You're about as clear as mud today."

"Is that an expression?"

"Yes." He paused, then picked up his box cutter. "Daphne …"

At that moment Morgan, the night manager, poked her head into the storeroom. "Daphne, I think you should leave early today. There's a lull in the storm, but it's supposed to get worse later. Just get home before there's a microburst or something."

Daphne nodded, waved to Karl, and left.

The parking lot looked eerie in the dim light. Daphne got in her car with an air of relief, but when it wouldn't start she felt ready to burst into tears. She got out again and stood uncertainly. Should she look under the hood? Would it tell her anything? She knew nothing about mechanical things. With a shock, she realized that she was the helpless female she had always despised in books.

Someone was coming; she squinted, then saw, to her horror, the man who had complained about the science fiction section, the man who had yelled at her and threatened to call her superiors. He recognized her, too, and seemed to be making his way toward her. "Shit," she said.

"Hey," a voice said. She turned to see John Baynor, the chef; he was trying to light a cigarette in the drizzle and finding it difficult. "You having trouble?" he asked, his eyes on his lighter.

"Yeah. My car won't start. Do you think you could take a look?"

He shrugged, gave up on his cigarette, stowed it in his shirt pocket. "I'm not the most mechanical guy around, but sure."

Daphne peered over her shoulder; to her horror, the man she thought of as 'that crazy guy' was a few cars down, apparently waiting. WAITING, and giving her the creeps.

John Baynor peeked around her raised hood. "I can't see anything wrong, but it's also so damn dark that it's hard to make things out."

"Yeah."

"You in Triple A or something?"

"Uh—no, but I think I have free roadside assistance through my insurance company."

"Great. If you want, I'll drop you at your place and you can get it towed."

Daphne hesitated. "I'm twenty minutes west. Is that out of your way?"

"Nah. I'm in Western Springs. That close to you?"

"Yes, that's great. Thanks so much, Mr. Baynor."

"John, please. You're not a kid anymore and I'm at an age where I feel sensitive about old man titles."

She laughed. "Okay."

She followed him through the lot to a blue Lexus parked under a large tree. She went to the passenger door and a flash of pain assaulted her temples. "Ow!" she yelled.

"Something wrong?"

"A headache. Out of nowhere."

"Let's get you home," he said, unlocking his door.

Don't go with him.

"What?"

"I didn't say anything."

"No—uh—sorry. The pain is confusing me."

Daphne, do not get in his car. He's a wrong one. He tampered with your engine.

"What?"

"Hey, are you okay?" He came around to her side, his face a picture of concern.

"Uh, yeah. You know what? I just remembered something I left in my car. I want to get it real quick."

"Just get it later. Look, the rain is about to come. We'll get soaked. Just hop in my car and you can retrieve it from the tow truck driver." His hand was on her arm.

"John, I need it now. I won't be a minute."

"Sure."

Daphne! Watch out!

She turned to see something in his hand, some sort of weapon, and she ran.

He caught up with her, grabbed her with his free hand, and she swung at him. Her fist connected with his eye, but he didn't seem to feel it. He was dragging her by her purse; she'd slipped the long strap over her head, and he was practically strangling her now. She was down, on the ground, and he was on top of her, choking her in earnest, then raising the strange little weapon and guiding it toward her neck . . .

Then he was pulled off of her; he flew up and away.

"Mom?" she cried.

There were sounds of a struggle; she sat up and saw the crazy science-fiction guy karate chopping John Baynor's hand, trying to make him drop his weapon. Kneeling on John Baynor's chest was Karl from shipping and receiving. He was punching Baynor in the face.

You're safe, Daphne.

There was such relief in those words that Daphne felt it too: a wild rush of something between laughter and tears, even as the first huge raindrop hit her face.

A police car showed up. The crazy guy helped Daphne to

her feet. "I saw him under your hood earlier. When I realized it was your car, I waited to see if you knew him. You seemed to, and then you walked behind that tree and I wasn't sure if it was okay. So I followed you."

"Thanks," Daphne said.

The police were prying Karl from the bloodied John Baynor. The crazy guy started telling the officers what he had witnessed. Karl gave Daphne a bear hug. It felt odd, hugging Karl from receiving, but also nice.

"Daphne, I couldn't stop worrying about you when you left. It's not like I didn't think you could handle some rain. I don't know, it's weird. It was relentless, like a voice in my head. I had to go after you for my own piece of mind."

"I understand," she said. He stopped hugging her, so she lifted his hand and held it. "Thanks."

He cares about you. He has for a long time. Her mother sounded surprised about this.

They stayed to speak to the police in the growing rain. Daphne watched in horror as they searched Baynor's car, found duct tape and knives in his trunk.

"That could be for anything, right?" Daphne said. "For a household project or something."

"Not the tazer in his hand, though," Karl said.

The police took their names, told them they could go find a dry place. Karl pulled out a cell phone and talked briefly to Morgan.

"Let me take you home," he said.

Daphne got into his car; no protests from her mother.

As they drove, Karl allowed her some quiet. Finally she said, "My mom says I should join a book group or something."

Karl looked at her. "Your mom who died?"

"Yes."

"I think I met her earlier."

"That's a distinct possibility."

"I think a book club sounds fun. Want to form one?"

"No spoilers, now."

"No spoilers." His face looked as content as Daphne felt despite her trauma.

"Mom?" she said in her mind.

I might be out of touch for a while . . . but the important thing is you know I'm here, right?

"I know."

Get rid of the erotica before Jason sells the house.

"I love you, Mom."

And get out of those wet things the minute you get home.

Fangs for the Memories

Lance Zarimba

"I bid you welcome," the *maitre d'* said with a Hungarian accent. His good-as-gold lapel nametag read *Lurch*.

"Why Billy Joe Jim Bob, I do declare, you really know how to treat a lady." Ima tickled her date's scruffy cheek as they followed the host like ducks in a row into the restaurant.

Peanut shells crunched underfoot as they made their way to the light at the end of the tunnel and found a booth in the back. "My little buck-a-roo. I'm sorry I freaked you out when you asked me if I wanted to get steaked tonight. My heart was in my throat." She batted her long, lush eyelashes at him.

"I didn't mean like in the 'pup tent' sense," Billy Joe Jim Bob said. "I was talking food, meat, like supper."

Lurch interrupted: "Duck soup is the special of the day, soup *du jour.* But what would you like to drink?"

Billy Joe Jim Bob puffed his chest. "Sky's the limit, honey. Shoot the moon. If it's on the menu, it's on the table. Fine as wine?"

"I never drink...wine," Ima said. "I worry I have champagne tastes on a beer budget."

"Honey, I don't want you climbing the walls, or chewing nails and spitting tacks. I'll pick up the tab. Whatever trips your trigger. I'm your man. Money don't buy you happiness and it don't grow on trees, but tonight, money is burning a hole in my pocket."

"A fool and his money are soon parted, but money makes the world go round. Lucky I'm a girl of simple tastes."

"I want a girl who tastes good," he said with a glimmer of hope in his eyes. He looked like his blood was boiling and something was crawling under his skin.

Lurch rolled his eyes. "I'll be back in two shakes of a lamb's tail." He split like a banana.

Ima licked her lips. "Alone at last."

A drunken couple sitting at the window table hooted and hollered. "You're pulling my leg, baby," said the blonde with over-processed hair. She bounced up and down like she had ants in her pants. The frog in a blender made like a jumping bean and twisted open the Venetian blind's control. A ray of sunlight cut between the blades like a knife through hot butter.

A single shaft of light washed over Ima.

Billy Joe Jim Bob turned his back to her and shouted, "That chaps my hide!"

In a split second, Ima's body *pffted* into a cloud of smoke, ashes to ashes, and dust to dust.

The blinds closed in the nick of time, and her body reformed with another *pfft*.

Billy Joe Jim Bob turned and looked at her in surprise.

Ima covered her mouth with her hand. "Oops, excuse me," was all she said.

"No need to get all bent out of shape, little lady. The same thing happens to me when I eat beans, baked beans, and ham. Beans, beans, the musical fruit. *Who-ee*, no one wants to be around me then. Especially if I'm drinking beer and eating pork rinds. I sound like I'm gonna blow a gasket."

Ima opened her mouth to explain but stopped. She waved her hand at him like she was swatting a fly. "Oh, you little joker. You're so sweet."

"What's good for the goose is good for the gander. Let's stop spinning our wheels and order so we can make tracks."

"I second that motion."

Lurch returned. "The ball is in your court." A small order pad took care of the business at hand. And he waited.

Silence from Ima.

"Time is running out," Lurch said. "My shift is ending soon, I'm ready to call it a day."

Grasping at straws, Billy Joe Jim Bob placed an order for two.

"When push comes to shove, you take charge," Ima said. "I like that in a man. I bet your bottom dollar you're firing on all cylinders tonight."

Billy Joe Jim Bob growled. He knew he had a sweet deal.

At the eleventh hour, Lurch laid it on the line. The food was plunked down in front of them.

"Just in the nick of time," Billy Joe Jim Bob said. "We were heading for the poorhouse. I heard their midnight special was quick as a wink."

"Better late than never," Lurch said, did an about face, and marched off like a good soldier.

Ima's raw steak oozed blood on the platter.

"Why don't you stick a fork in it and see if it's done," Billy Joe Jim Bob suggested.

She moved the small potatoes to the side and dangled a carrot in front of him. "You get all worked up. Don't sweat it."

Billy Joe Jim Bob pointed at her plate. "You can tell a good cut of meat when you chew the fat and it gets bigger in your mouth."

The band played on.

"Music of the Night," Ima said. "My favorite song from *Phantom*." Her hands trailed down her hourglass figure.

Billy Joe Jim Bob's eyes popped out of their sockets. Her fabric hugged every curve and formed a second skin. She was stacked. He licked his lips. "Check please."

Lurch made his last-ditch effort. "Ready for your just

desserts? A piece of cake? It ain't over until the fat lady sings."

"Chocolate is too rich for my blood," Ima said.

"Easy as pie?"

"The crust is hard to swallow, so ice cream. I'll take it nice and easy." She smiled.

"Good call, Madame." Lurch was happy as a lark for making the sale of the century.

When the bottom fell out of dessert, Lurch returned. He set the small black plastic tray on the table. "That's the ticket. Time to pay the piper."

Billy Joe Jim Bob paid up and the couple exited stage right, pausing for a second wind outside the restaurant door. "Watch your step, someone blew his wad." A pink blob of bubble gum stared up at them.

Once they were in the clear, Ima said, "My shoes wouldn't stand a prayer knee deep in the hoopla. You're my hero."

"Ma'am, you do a man proud, but I don't want to move too fast."

"Why sir, I do declare. I'm not sweet sixteen and never been kissed. I'm as old as dirt." With a whiplash smile, she said: "Tell me what you want."

"Coffee, tea, or me? Your place or mine?"

"I live over the hill." She imagined the place she slept and tried to think outside the box.

"My place is just around the horn." He offered his arm.

"Sounds like a plan was used when they organized the neighborhood." She took an arm and a leg and headed south.

They laughed all the way to the bank, and turned right on Elm Street. Following in his footsteps, she danced in the moonlight and howled at the moon. They walked all over the map and finally stopped at his house and met eye to eye. "Are you sure you want to come in?"

"I'm not a fly-by-night kind of gal." She upped the ante and sweetened the pot.

"Age before beauty?" The keypad glowed in the dark. "Wanna

push my buttons?" he asked.

"Do or die time?" she questioned as her eyebrows rose. But sugar wouldn't melt in her mouth; it bubbled over the top.

They were in the black when they entered the house. "I hope you like dogs, but don't rattle his cage. We'd have a better night if we let sleeping dogs lie. Bubba is a loving creature, but he'd give you a tongue lashing with his kisses. He's a baby and would never bite the hand that fed him."

"I'll follow your lead." She cooed like a dove. Soon she was in like Flynn. Lara Flynn Boyle had nothing on her.

A rogue's gallery of family photos filled the living room. She looked at the writing on the wall and her fingers pointed to a picture of a red barn. "A picture's worth a thousand words. This wall spills a lot of secrets."

Billy Joe Jim Bob cuddled up to her side. "It's my Dad's ranch. My dad, Pete Billy Bob Paul, wrote lyrics and he bought it for a song—one that hit the top of the charts with a bullet. But as luck would have it, he had horrible asthma and hay fever. And for Pete's sake he had to stop ranching and sell. I bought the farm."

"And what about this one?" She referred to a picture with a man and a deer caught in the headlights.

"It was a quick buck, but the buck stops here, right where my brother shot it. That was our first season in the Sun County Boy Scouts."

Ima spun on her heels to face him. "Let's get down to business." She took the shirt right off his back.

They moved to the bedroom, and her every wish was his command. In a split-second, Billy Joe Jim Bob was spread eagle.

Ima followed him to the bed, but kicked the bucket of beers cooling by the side.

"Sorry," he apologized. "I only have one nightstand by the bed. The other one is in the garden, pushing up daisies. Say your prayers, it's time to sink or swim." He rolled over and bit the dust on the pillow. "If you scratch my back I'll scratch yours."

Her hand ran over the headboard. "Ouch," she said and pulled her hand away quick as a flash.

"It's natural wood. Its bark is worse than its bite. We may need to wrap you up."

"It cuts like a knife, but look—no blood," Ima showed him, hands down. She moved closer and slipped between the sheets.

Her canine teeth slowly extended.

"You're looking a little long in the tooth," he said.

"Receding gum lines."

"You're cold as the grave. I'll warm you up."

"Go belly up." She smiled and motioned him closer. "It's not over until it's over." Her long slender fingers trailed down his chest.

"You make my blood boil, even though you are as cold as a witch's—" He exhaled and stopped. The scent of garlic hung in the air. "I'd better hide the salami I had for supper." He bounced off the bed to brush his pearly whites.

"Wait. I need to come clean," she said.

"You want to take a bath? We could work each other into a lather."

The final unveiling had arrived. Ima couldn't take the easy way out; she faced him head on. "Honey, you do know I'm a vampire. I cast no reflection. I'm one of the undead, a blood-sucking fiend."

He laughed. "Like that's a no-brainer. Can we say yes?"

Now it was Ima with the wool pulled over her eyes. "You knew? And yet, you still invited me into your hearth and home?"

"Ima, I'm a man. I'm horny as a toad. I'd bang anything that moves. Why wouldn't I take you home? You're one hot sex machine."

"Love is blind," she said.

"No, Ima, you're beautiful. Maybe not being able to see your-self in the mirror is only skin deep, and maybe you have a face only a mother could love, but I could learn to love your face."

"Fangs and all?"

"Fangs and all."

"I can cook too."

"So what's for breakfast?" he asked.

"I think we'll be makin' bacon."

They kissed. And then her lips and fangs moved down his neck, searching for the right spot, finding it.

His body slumped in her arms.

"Melts in your mouth, not in your hands," she said. "So at the end of the day never underestimate the power of a woman."

All's well that ends well.

Slurp!

L. K. Rigel

He held her close—so close, she didn't know anymore where she ended and he began. Crazy to deny him anything now; they had become virtually the same being.

Was that a noise? I looked up from my laptop, which provided the only light in the living room. Another day had slipped away, lost to world-building. In the kitchen, I switched on the burner under the kettle, my hero and heroine still in my head, still locked in a battle of wits. Both losing, ha.

The WIP consumed me, in a good way. My muse had come back. I was on a roll.

Kill your babies. That's been the command from the time of Moloch. Not with this one. Move along, nothing to kill here, ha. Like everybody says: with the bad stuff you struggle and struggle; the good stuff writes itself.

It happened with *Mock Me, Baby*. My first novel flowed as if my muse had dictated it directly. Three agents offered on the same day, and within two weeks it sold at auction. There was a real advance, the kind you get, yanno, in advance. I bought my little cottage on three acres down a dirt lane. I bought it for the solitude. I thought I could write there.

The doorbell rang.

I was right. There had been a noise.

My muse left me when I wasn't paying attention, some-time between *Mock Me's* laydown day and the third printing. I quit feeding him, so he quit feeding me. The second book took forever and never earned out. My agent dropped me on the third book. She said she read it, but she didn't. The other two agents forgot my name at nationals—after trying to steal me every goddamn year before that. Both emailed later: While my latest project sounded intriguing, it wasn't right for their list at this time.

I see one of them on Twitter all the time now, always bitch-ing about authors.

The bell rang again, and that sick feeling swarmed over me, the sense that I owed somebody something, but hadn't put it on my calendar and forgot to do it. It happened less often since my muse had come back and I'd written three books. But when it hit, it was merciless. I opened the door, and a trick-or-treater held out a plastic pumpkin bucket. I'd forgotten it was Halloween.

Last year I only had two trick-or-treaters, one early and one way too late and too old. This year I didn't bother to decorate. Didn't buy candy.

I told the kid to wait a minute and went back to the kitchen for some chocolate parfait Nips. What the hell. I threw an unopened box into his pumpkin.

When I closed the door, the nausea got worse. I'd done something wrong. Morphorlis was not amused. I felt his anger bubbling up from the basement, but I couldn't go down there. I had nothing to give him. My hero and heroine still hated each other. I was glad he was back—gawd, I was glad. But did he have to be so voracious?

You have to do more for less. Everybody says so. Publishers don't fund book tours, so you have to hire your own publicist. Lose weight. Be younger. Be clever online. Have a good attitude. Contribute more. Expect less. With the last book, the advance was quartered and drawn over eighteen months. I spent it all on promotion and web design. Ha. Quartered and drawn. I made a note to tweet that.

Anon is my Twitter name. I mean it in the Shakespearean, *I'll-be-there-soon* sense. Not anonymous. Most people don't get it.

I was trying. I blogged, I tweeted, I wrote and wrote and wrote.

It never lasted! The last book took six months, working every day. I put it out on Smashwords, and Morphorlis just grinned and smacked his lips and made that sound. *Slurp*. Six months, and he devoured all my work like a piece of cake. Then he batted his eyelashes and wanted more.

I was deluding myself: Morphorlis wasn't a muse. He was a demon.

Still, I wanted to please him. I needed to. I had to feed him so he could feed me.

But it was a symbiosis made in hell. He would consume her if she let him; and she wanted to let him. She was a sick puppy.

He actually whined. He didn't like the way the story was going. I would have to kill a baby or two after all. But I loved this one. I loved every word.

The doorbell rang again. "Twik-ah-tweat." It was a darling little thing with round brown eyes and innocent expectation.

"And what are you?" I knew, but I'd let her tell me. In the basement Morphorlis made demanding grunts.

"A baby kitteh."

A baby. The demon grunting was insistent, frantic. I lifted her easily. Would he be satisfied with something so slight? As I threw the sacrifice down to Morphorlis, the nausea turned to terror. What if it did make him happy? After all my blood and tears poured out over so many pages, I couldn't bear it if he were satisfied by some accidental, found object.

As I closed the basement door, I heard *slurp!* I pictured his batting eyelashes. Not enough. I smiled.

Okay, it was mere *schadenfreude*. But dammit, I was relieved. Giddy. Energized, rededicated. What had I been thinking? Of course found objects wouldn't do. It had to be something I created myself. Morphorlis wasn't a demon after all.

She was sick, and he was her healer...

I don't remember hearing the banging on the door. Or later, the approaching sirens. I had just checked Twitter and noticed I had two new, non-porno followers. Then four uniformed policemen were staring at me, guns drawn. Another officer restrained a writhing young woman dressed like a cat with a painted feline nose and glued-on whiskers.

The scene was a gift from Morphorlis. I turned to my WIP.

"Where is she!" The catwoman blubbered, messy and frantic. She squirmed in the officer's muscular arms. She had to break loose, get to her daughter. "Where is she!"

No, that's not it. Put the daughter in later. More muscle.

She had to break loose. She had to. But it was impossible to ignore his rock-hard chest as he tightened his grip around her waist. She searched his twinkling blue eyes. Yes, he was doing his job, but it was more than that. He loved her. She was certain of it now.

I think I confused my stories there for a while.

A woman in the seat behind the defense table averts her eyes every time I look at her, but I don't think she believes I'm dangerous. *Click, click, click.* She works a laptop with a mifi plugged in. Liveblogging. Good for her, creating content.

My lawyer comes in through the gallery. He doesn't look at anyone until he gets past the swinging, hip-high double doors on his way to the defense table. He's a solid, short-haired, ex-football-player-looking guy. I swear his suit set him back three grand easy.

"Betsy Betzi called me this morning." He looks over his shoulder and searches the crowd behind us. "She wants a meeting."

"*The* Betsy Betzi. The agent."

"Superagent, according to her. She gave me the idea she was in town."

I know who she is. Betsy-if-you-don't-hear-back-I-don't-want-you Betzi. I've got livebloggers and interview requests. All of a sudden, I'm marketable. I can't afford this lawyer. The agreement is, he gets half of any deals he can spin out of this. I didn't tell him Morphorlis had vanished, but I did say I haven't been able to write. He says that won't be a problem.

The bailiff steps in front of us. "All rise!"

It takes ages to get to an actual murder trial, but the courtroom is packed for my preliminary hearing, and the judge takes the bench in a red-faced snit. I'm famous. I was known once by people in the industry. A contingent from my old fan club has arisen from its grave and claimed the front row behind the district attorney's table.

"Both counsel with me. Now." The judge motions the DA and my guy into his chambers and growls at everyone else to stay put.

A fangirl separates from the club, her eyes on the prize. Me.

"Can I have your autograph?" She sticks a disintegrating paperback in my face. "I have all your books." It smells like cigarettes, the only clean spot a neon-bright sticker from a used bookstore.

Someone else maneuvers in front of her, the clicker liveblogger lady. "You're Anon, aren't you?"

Do I know her online? Are we close?

"O. M. G." The middle-aged fangirl squees. She raises her hands to her cohorts and makes jazz hands, mouthing: *I told you! This is Anon!* Gawd. They all follow me.

I'm still holding the disgusting mass market. Did I really write a book called *The Avante Gardner*? What a title. No wonder it didn't earn out.

The liveblogger woman sits down and bangs on her keyboard. She's outing me on Twitter. Fine. *Note to self: ask lawyer to check how many followers I have after today.*

The bailiff tells us to sit down. As I turn around I hear—or I think I hear—something I haven't heard since that night. I swing around to look at the blogger woman. The *click-click* stops; she freezes, her eyes still lowered. She won't look up, but she heard it too. In fact, I'm sure it was for her benefit. He's her muse now.

Slurp!

Graveyard Soul Sucker

Kelly Lynn Parra

"This is creepy." I scanned the dark grounds of Meadow Brook Graveyard. The patch of land was so rejected it didn't even warrant a caretaker. Weeds towered over gravestones. The air reeked of skunk and mold, and wind blew the rusted gate entrance back and forth like a haunted violin.

Danny squeezed my hand in reassurance. "We're just having some fun, Vada."

"Midnight on All Hallows Eve at a graveyard? Kinda high school don't you think?"

"Maybe. Just because you're a big college girl now…" Danny leaned down and kissed me. "I'll make it up to you later."

I smiled and wrapped my arms around his warm body. "Promise?"

Pauly Jones, who everyone called Jones, said in his best psychotic whisper voice from behind me, *"You're not scared of a dead serial killer are you?"*

I didn't let on that his words sent a shiver down my back. I pulled away from Danny. "Shut it, Jones."

"Aw, you've hurt my feelings, Vada. I think I might cry."

"Leave her alone." Danny sighed, likely tired of refereeing our verbal tennis matches.

"Yes, sir, Danny Sir!" Jones saluted and jogged his big form ahead to the other couple in the group, searching for a two hundred year-old grave.

"Such a jerk," I said under my breath.

"Just the way Jones is. Always been like that. Always will be."

"Can you just take me home, Danny?" I rubbed my neck. It felt like someone was staring into my back.

Jones let out an irritating whoop. "Here it is!"

"Soon. Come on." Danny pulled me along to where the trio was huddled.

Jones's flashlight illuminated a tombstone. The ancient marker was tilted and chipped, the engravings barely legible.

"Here lies John Peter Montgomery, Graveyard Soul Sucker," said Jones.

"It doesn't say that," Bobby said on a laugh.

"Nah, but it'd be cool if it did."

"What's the story with this dude?"

Jones shined the flashlight under his chin, making his face glow like a ghost in the dark. "Legend goes that Montgomery was one of the worst serial killers of his time. Said he killed all kinds of peeps to take their souls into his body by black magic. Like he had twenty-five souls trapped inside him when he was captured and hung."

"That's bull," I countered. I tried to sound brave, but it's kind of tough when you're standing over the grave of a serial killer.

Jones slipped out an inch-thick pocketbook, waving it in the air. "It's all here in this old book I found at the geezer's shop."

"So why can he only come alive on Halloween?" Danny asked.

"Says a witch fell in love with the soul sucker. He didn't return the vibe, so she put a curse on him. For all eternity he can only come alive midnight to midnight on Halloween to eat as many souls as he wants if you perform this ritual." He tapped the book.

"That's so romantic," a girl named Jenny said. We all stared at her. "Well, it is, sort of. So what do we do, Jones?"

"Spread the five candles around the tombstone like the five points of a star. Hurry up, it's almost midnight."

"Holy shit, Jones! What's with the knife, homie?" Danny wanted to know.

My eyes widened. Jones had seriously lost it.

The idiot laughed, holding a five-inch hunting knife. "Says you gotta use blood."

"Your own, I hope," I muttered. Danny squeezed my hand, this time in warning.

"Just a few drops will do us." Jones sliced his own plump thumb with a flinch, and my gut trembled as blood dripped slowly onto the grave. Tiny pins danced along my skin. A cloud floated across the moon, the shadow darkening the tombstone.

"It's midnight," Jenny whispered. "Nothing's happening."

Bobby chuckled nervously.

Jones started trembling, his flashlight shaking.

"What's wrong with him?" I asked, all nervous.

Danny stepped next to his friend. "Jones, stop messing around, homie."

Gurgling sounds erupted from Jones's mouth, and he fell to his knees, convulsing.

"Somebody help him!" *Oh crap, oh crap.* We crowded around, not knowing what the hell to do.

Then he just stopped, falling flat on his back.

Still as death.

My hand slapped to my mouth.

Bobby cursed into the cold night air. The sound of the grave-yard gate fell silent.

Jones jumped to his feet and let out a horror-flick death scream.

Everyone leaped back. I screeched with Jenny.

Jones busted up laughing, grabbing his gut. "Oh-oh-oh man, your faces—totally classic."

"You jerk, Jones!" I shouted. "Let's get out of here, Danny," I pulled on his arm.

"That was messed up, Jones," Danny said, and turned with us to leave.

"Aw, come on! It's all in fun!"

"Whatever, man," Bobby called out. "You suck graveyard dirt, asshole!"

Suddenly, fast footfalls sounded from behind us.

"Freaking run!!"

Jones again. We didn't bother to look back.

"Whatever, Jones," Danny called out.

"Jesus, RUN!!"

Annoyed, I let go of Danny and turned around—and found myself face to face with a dark form. His clothes were tattered. His skull was exposed, and worms wiggled through his nose and empty eye sockets.

Not a man—a monster.

A decaying zombie.

I was too terrified to scream.

❖

The zombie reached toward me with skeletal fingers, gurgling through his rotted teeth.

I stood frozen in panic.

Then it was just…gone. Speeding away like a bolt of lightning.

"Holy damn mother-freaking shit," Danny hissed from behind me.

Someone yelled, "Get the hell away from me!"

I jerked to the right. The zombie gripped Bobby by the head. Bobby swung his arms out, hitting the creature, and his fist sunk into the rotting corpse's chest. He brought out his hand covered with black slime. Bobby cursed. The zombie lowered his mouth toward Bobby's face. Something green and wispy floated out of his mouth into the zombie's.

Bobby screamed and screamed. Then went limp, liquid dripping from his mouth.

Blood.

The zombie dropped him like a rag doll, stretched his arms wide, and roared like a freaking bear.

"Holy shit." Danny latched onto my hand and we rushed toward the gate.

The zombie zoomed past us, blocking the entrance. We pivoted and spotted Jones huddling behind a large statue. We dove down with him.

Breath rushed out of my mouth. My gut turned like a spin cycle.

Sick. Sick. *Feel sick.*

"Shit, Jones, how the hell is this happening?" Danny asked.

Jones shook his head, eyes wide. "D-don't know."

"Where's Jenny?" I ask.

"Damn, I can't see her," Danny whispered.

"Jones, how do we stop it?" I demanded, fighting tears.

"I-I didn't read that far. I didn't think this would really work!"

Jenny's scream pierced the night.

"Oh God," Jones cried. Really cried.

"We have to call for help!" The zombie was taking us out one by one. "Jones, just give me the book!"

Danny cursed. "My cell's not getting service out here."

Jones, the ass, threw the book at me. I grabbed his flashlight and skimmed the pages. "Come on, come on."

"Where is it?" Danny whispered, craning his neck around the statue.

Heart pounding, I read as fast as I could. "I think I found something. We have to go back to the grave. Say some words, and use blood again. From a...female."

"All right," Danny murmured. "Okay. Jones, we have to distract the zombie."

Jones shook his head like a wet dog. "HELL NO."

"Jones, you're the one that got us into this stupid mess."

"I told you—it was supposed to be a joke! Danny, you gotta believe me, bro!"

I skimmed the pages, my fingers trembling. "Um...if you grab some of his grave dirt and throw it at him, it's supposed to protect you from him."

Jones shut his eyes. "Oh God."

"Jones," Danny whispered. "We'll run to the grave. Grab some dirt and then you run left, and I'll run right. It'll give Vada time to do the ritual."

"Danny..." I said, really scared.

He kissed me, quick. His lips were cold. "You can do it, Vada."

I was shivering, but I nodded. "Please be careful."

Danny flashed the grin that most girls swooned over. "See you soon."

❖

Peering around the statue, I watched them run toward the zombie's grave. My pulse hammered as I prayed into the night.

The zombie swooped behind them, gaining speed. He grabbed Danny by the arm and my breath caught. I stood as Danny scooped up dirt and threw it at the zombie's rotten head. The zombie screeched and sped away.

Jones was piling dirt into his pockets like it was freaking gold. I ran toward them. Danny had to haul Jones to his feet to get him going, and then they took off in opposite directions from the grave.

Sweat broke from my pores. I fell to my knees. Took the knife Jones had used and sliced my hand. Too deep. I hissed as blood splashed the grave.

I heard Jones shout.

Tears stung my eyes.

I read the words from the book. Something changed...shifted. Like a veil dropping away. The book fell from my fingers. Cold air rushed against me. The passage flowed from my lips in a language I didn't understand. Something stormed through my body like wild fire. I gasped.

The zombie appeared in front of me. Wind buffeted him. He reached out to me in a way I didn't expect. Touching my face gently. Slime dripped down my cheek.

Danny called my name, but I couldn't look at him. Too afraid.

"Go away…forever," I whispered, "Just go away."

The zombie sank into the dirt, the ground swallowing him. His mouth opened in what looked like surprise. Dirt filled his mouth, then his eye sockets, until he was gone. The gravestone cracked down the center, crumbling into pieces.

I couldn't move.

Danny nearly knocked me down as he rushed to me. He grabbed my face to meet my eyes. "*Vada.*"

"It's over," I said.

He pulled me into a hug.

❖

Lights flashed across my face. Jones, Danny and I, leaned against a sheriff's Bronco, wrapped in blankets. We were the only ones to survive. Bobby and Jenny were dead. The zombie had killed them. He'd taken their souls.

I felt numb.

The Sheriff wouldn't believe us. He thought we were dropping acid. They thought Bobby and Jenny had overdosed, because they were just lifeless. No visible wounds.

"They don't believe us," Jones whined. "I mean, the proof is in the freaking book." He flipped through the pages.

"I wouldn't have believed it either, Jones, if I hadn't experienced this," Danny said, tired. "Damn, at least we're alive." He pulled me close for a moment. "I'm going to see if we can get out of here." He looked at me. "Sure you're okay?"

I nodded and Danny walked away.

"Vada?" Jones said, strangely.

I wouldn't look at him. "What?"

"It says here in the book the only females that can get the

soul sucker back in the grave…"

I finally met his eyes, finishing his sentence. "Are those descended from the witch."

Jones's breaths filtered from his mouth fast and short. "But how? How did you know?"

"I didn't. I just took a chance that it might work."

"But—but—but." Jones's eyes rolled back in his head before he toppled face first into graveyard dirt.

He'd fainted.

"Yeah, tripped me out too," I said quietly.

She Came
on the October Wind

Jason Evans

OCTOBER 21

Natalie stirred her apple-spiced tea.

Outside, gusts whipped yellow tornados in leaves, and ashen clouds marched across the sky.

The quiet house creaked. Natalie sprinkled in more sugar and watched the tiny crystals wiggle and melt away. Her thoughts hovered where the tea became dark and bottomless.

When a black cat landed on the window ledge, Natalie didn't jump or spill. The syrup of her thoughts shed slowly. Tired. Like the hanging drops on her leaky faucet before they fell.

Her cup steamed as the cat curled against the window frame. She'd never seen the animal before. Green eyes blinked, and its mouth whispered a muted meow.

How odd. How very odd.

Natalie didn't move. Or tried not to move. But her hand twitched under the weight of the tea, and the animal whisked away in a ripple of black.

OCTOBER 23

Natalie stirred her apple-spiced tea.

She watched the sunlight flutter on the surviving leaves. Her gaze dwelled on the small pile of dog food on the window ledge. Untouched for two days.

The cat wasn't coming back. That was obvious. It would've been offended by dog food anyway. Damn finicky cats.

Of course, the kibble was old. Natalie had babysat her mother's Chihuahua more than eight months ago.

Still, she watched.

Not much else to do.

She emptied her cup down to drops and spun the tea leaves into meaningless patterns. Her thoughts wandered until a shiver of black slipped onto the sill.

Natalie's breath caught.

The cat flattened.

Eyes so intense. Unwavering. It glared at the food.

Then, the spell broke. It sauntered over and ate.

Afterward, it perched like an owl, and Natalie eased closer and touched the glass. It didn't flee this time. It rubbed luxuriously where her fingerprints pressed.

Natalie smiled.

"Hi there," she said.

OCTOBER 25

Natalie burned her tongue on her apple-spiced tea.

Her mother was on the phone.

"What do you mean?" Natalie said. "Of course I let it in. Just for a minute. Just to say hello. It's a gorgeous cat."

A fresh pile of food sat on the windowsill. Cat food this time. The bag for the Chihuahua had gone out with yesterday's trash.

Her mother took her disapproving tone.

"No. Not really," Natalie said, half listening. "Nope."

She glanced at where she'd cracked the window open. Where the cat first nudged its head into her hand.

Natalie interrupted. "You know what's strange? I've been thinking about something. Something I'd forgotten. A story we used to tell each other."

Her mother asked who Natalie meant by *we*.

Natalie felt herself go pale.

She fumbled to change the subject. Trick-or-treating coming up soon. Whether her mother would expect a lot of kids again.

Her mother hated Halloween. She claimed scrubby kids got bused into the neighborhood and cleaned up all the candy.

When the monologue finally ended, her mother asked if Natalie would be doing something different.

"No," Natalie said. "I don't even decorate."

She glanced around the house.

Boring. Dusty.

Empty.

"It always felt like too much of a bother," she said. "Who am I going to do it for, anyway?"

Her gaze drifted to the forest beyond the window. A deep forest. Deep enough for someone to disappear.

"I even turn out all my lights on Halloween," she said. "I hide in my room with a book light. Nobody even bothers to soap my windows."

Natalie looked down at the table.

For the first time in ages, ashamed.

OCTOBER 26

Natalie nestled on the couch with her apple-spiced tea.

Afternoon weighed on the window. A knitting-needle wind clicked in the branches.

The sash stood open. No more than four inches. Enough for the breeze to lift a few papers and float them down to the floor.

Natalie set the tea aside and closed her eyes.

Her mind tiptoed out into the quiet.

She wandered through years of clutter back to purer times. Unstained. When cobwebs hadn't collected in the corners of her life.

She remembered crunching crispy leaves. She remembered school evenings. Reading on her bed. Pages cut by dark and lamplight.

She remembered Amanda.

Amanda had been a year and half older than Natalie. Tall. Flowing hair. A strange lust in her eyes. So darkly dazzling she could bewitch an empty room.

I have to go, Amanda had said. Sister to sister. Sixteen years ago.

Natalie, the confidante. The partner in crime. But bathing in Amanda's shadow. Bewitched, like the empty room.

I really have to go.

The memory hurt. Even with the music of Amanda's voice. But the sound infused her.

It would not be separated.

Natalie, you can't come with me. Even if I wanted you to.

Natalie clenched her fists and tried to squeeze the pain of Amanda away.

Then, something touched Natalie's shoulder. Just a small touch. Like a tiny, tentative hand. Natalie's eyes opened.

The black cat perched on the edge of the couch next to her. Whiskers twitched an inch from Natalie's ear. The cat had come in through the window.

Two slow blinks veiled the green eyes.

A motion of love.

Or apology.

October 27

Natalie drank her apple-spiced tea.

The sleeping cat swelled and shrank on top of the radiator. Natalie's nervous hand sweated on the phone.

"Mom, can I ask you something? I know we don't talk about Amanda. Ever. I know we like to pretend that she didn't exist. No, let me finish. I have to ask you. Does she ever contact you? Do you ever talk to her? Or hear from her? Ever? Do you have any idea where she is?"

Silence.

"Any idea at all?"

More silence.

"Mom?"

The whispered reply was low and vicious. Curses for an ungrateful daughter.

"Look, I understand you're upset. But don't you ever want to find her? She's your *daughter*. No matter how much you fought with her. No matter how much you hated her."

A denial. More hard words.

Natalie turned to the sleeping cat.

"Well, *I've* tried to find her. Lots of times. Even though she obviously doesn't give a crap about me. Even though *I'm* the easiest person in the world to find. With no married name. Living less than 20 miles from where I was born. But that doesn't really matter. Not now. It's not right, Mom. We should know where she is."

Her mother scoffed.

"It's just not right."

OCTOBER 28

The cat followed each Halloween decoration in Natalie's hand. It mewed at a jack-o'-lantern. Nudged a billowy ghost with its nose.

"My mother wanted to throw all this away," Natalie said. "I saved it from the trash. See? That's her psycho handwriting on the box."

The cat meowed.

Yeah. No sane person wrote like that.

Natalie chose perfect places for all of the old favorites. "That looks much better, doesn't it?" she said, surveying the room.

She stood with her hands on her hips. The cat blinked.

"Yes. Loads better. I just needed a little motivation." She smiled. "Thanks."

She cleaned up the packing papers. When the phone rang and her mother's number flashed on the display, she let it go to the machine.

OCTOBER 29

Natalie drank her apple-spiced tea.

The cat balled itself on her lap. Tail twitching. Natalie set down the old book of ghost stories that she and Amanda used to read to each other.

"You know, my sister Amanda and I used to make up stories," Natalie said. "I was just thinking about our favorite."

The cat blinked.

"We'd pretend that a black cat would come to our window. Kind of funny, huh? A magical cat. We used to have lots of stories like that. But this story was special. The cat would come in the middle of the night on Halloween. We'd only see its glowing eyes at the window."

Natalie stroked the cat's ears down to the tip of the tail.

"We used to pretend it was meant for us."

The green eyes closed.

"It would give us powers. Witch powers. We would do dark things, beautiful things, amazing things. We would cast spells. We could read minds."

Natalie grinned. "Sometimes Amanda pretended to be the cat, and sometimes it would be me. Mostly me. Amanda liked my cat voice. And Amanda made such a better witch than me. She dreamed up the most devilish spells. I loved just to listen. I could listen to her forever."

Natalie remembered curling in Amanda's lap. Purring.

She looked down. Knowing how the cat felt.

And for the first time, knowing how Amanda had felt.

OCTOBER 30

Natalie gulped the coffee black. The punch of caffeine rumbled to her fingers flying on the computer keyboard.

Directories. People pages. Names. Schools. Work. Networks. Photos. Videos. Updates. Uploads. Music lists. Book lists.

Obituaries.

The cat watched as Natalie fired through search after search, but no trace, no trace, no trace.

Her eyes stung.

❖

That night, Natalie dreamed of sitting at the kitchen table the morning after Amanda ran away. She dreamed of her father. Red-faced. Anger nailing him into silence. Her mother with her restless hands and machete tongue.

Natalie, sixteen years old, started to ask, where, why, but a fist into the table crumpled her voice.

In the dream, Amanda spoke from the darkness draped above the room. Above her beaten shape at the table.

Sweet, sweet Natalie. Don't cry.

But Natalie cried. Then, and now.

I was wrong. I was wrong to leave you.

Again, something brushed Natalie's cheek.

She lurched up into the early morning silence.

Outside her second story window, glowing eyes hovered in the blackness. But when she blinked, they were gone.

Natalie planted a shaking hand on the mattress and clicked on the lamp. Paper crinkled in her fingertips.

She lifted a choppy note lying beside her thigh. It looked like she'd scratched it while she slept.

An address. Number and street. San Francisco, California.

And a name. Tammany.

Natalie gaped.

Two rows of dimples crossed her comforter toward the closed window.

A perfect pattern for paws.

HALLOWEEN

Natalie booked the flight online and boarded six hours later. She crunched a single bag into the overhead compartment and buckled in. The clouds slid under her for hours until the plane landed in California.

She drove a rental car forty minutes to the address she'd written down. Not to a house. Not an apartment. As evening began to weigh, she pulled into the parking lot of a hospital and tried to quiet her shaking.

Under the rows of featureless grey windows, she walked. Automatic doors swished open, and an old woman at the information desk glanced up. In the lonely light of the computer at 3:30 that morning, Natalie had found the name of the hospital when she typed the address from her feathery note. Not until 7:05 had she been able to get a live person to answer the phone. Now, she already knew where to go.

"I'm looking for Room 311," she said.

The woman smiled and pointed over her shoulder. "Elevators are ahead and to your left. Just go up to the third floor and follow the signs for the room numbers."

Natalie thanked her and clicked across the floor. The silver doors opened to harsh light.

When she stepped out, the third floor murmured with the sound of nurses and monitors. Down the hall, an alarm chattered. Natalie drifted to the right and marched along the rooms. She stopped at 311. Inside, a dark-haired man napped at the far bedside. Past the curtain, Natalie saw the hands of the person under the sheets.

The man seemed to sense her presence and stirred. His forehead wrinkled.

"Mr. Tammany?" Natalie said.

He shook his head. "No. This is Amanda Tammany's room, though. Are you looking for her?"

Natalie nodded.

She advanced and the view of the person grew. She saw arms, one of them black and blue. She saw a chest quivering with a weak breath. She saw a face swollen and cut.

But the hair. Even matted, she recognized the beautiful, rich hair.

"Amanda?" she whispered.

The woman slept on. No twitch of recognition. Stillness too profound, too complete. Natalie noticed the lack of books, crossword puzzles, TV remote, laptop, magazines, and any other random stuff. Just monitors, dressings, and a lifeless face.

Natalie felt her knees buckling.

She collapsed into a chair.

"I'm sorry," the man said, confused. "Do I know you?" He stood. "I don't recognize—Do you need a tissue? Here."

"Are you...are you her husband?" Natalie managed.

"No. I'm Nathan McFarland. We're together. I mean, we live together."

Natalie stared at the woman lying in the bed. So apart from her. So foreign.

Yet not foreign.

"Do you work with Amanda?" he said.

Natalie shook her head. Without build-up, without fanfare, she simply said, "I'm her sister."

He stepped back. Troubled. "Wait. She told me she didn't have any family."

Despite her sobs, Natalie chuckled.

"Her sister?" he said again.

She nodded.

"I, I didn't know," he said.

He gripped his forehead. She stared at this woman Amanda had become.

"What happened?" she said.

"Car accident."

"When?"

"Two weeks ago. October 21st."

He sat hard.

"What's wrong with her?" she said.

"Head injury," he said. "Really bad."

"How bad?"

"The first night we actually thought she was going to be fine.

Everything was encouraging. Her vital signs were strong. She was even talking. But then the swelling started. In her brain. They even opened her skull to relieve the pressure. But nothing worked."

Yes. Just a husk of a body lying there.

"We lost her," he said. "She's been brain dead ever since."

Still, the words slapped.

The next tissue was for him. He hid it well, but took a minute to dab and compose. "I've been staying with her," he said. "Ever since they removed the respirator. They're making her comfortable. Giving her water. But that's all."

Too late. Much too late.

"I'm sorry," he said. "I'm so sorry. But we had to make a decision. If I had known—We would—But I had to decide. It was all on me. And she wouldn't have—"

"No," Natalie said. "You were right." She could see Amanda the way she used to look. Eyes never wavering for a second. "Amanda would have wanted it this way."

HALLOWEEN NIGHT

Natalie stood outside in the soft glow of the hospital lights. Over in the town streets, trick-or-treaters laughed and ran between houses. A ghost and witch passed under a streetlight. Some kind of demon followed. Natalie smiled, remembering the candy and cold October air.

Then, once again, the smile faded. An hour earlier, she'd watched Amanda take her last breath.

Natalie ran her fingers through her hair. She wanted to leave, to run, but had nowhere to go. The storm of emotions scoured her numb. She tried to watch the children again. To travel far away from there.

Something crinkled in the leaves behind her.

A blackness flowed along the ground into the murky light. Eyes blinked, regarding her with a mix of intensity and calm. A black cat.

Natalie let out her breath.

"Well, hello," she said.

It sprang and landed in her arms. She nearly fell backward in shock.

But the cat was undeterred. It wormed in.

Natalie gaped. Already, it draped its head over her forearm.

She tried to get a clear look at the face. Could it be the same cat? For a moment, she forgot about the thousands of miles from home.

It tipped its head as footsteps approached.

"There you are," Nathan said. "I've been looking for you."

"I was out here."

"The funeral home people arrived," he said. "They're going to be taking her soon."

The facade broke again, and he was sobbing.

The cat purred in her arms. A paw flexed, and claws poked into the tender back of her hand.

She jolted. Not from the ten little needles, not from the pain, but from a sudden thunder of power through her wrist, her forearm, her punched-open brain. Natalie looked down into lightening flashing in the cat's eyes.

"Amanda," she whispered.

Nathan misunderstood. "I know," he said, crying. "I know."

The blast of power fueled a new awareness. Natalie felt his hitching breaths. His muscles. The convergence of primordial energies sleeping between his legs.

With a circle of her hand, Natalie pulled some of the energy from him, smoothed it, and painted it in sharper hues. She pushed, and the wordless spell enveloped him.

His breath caught, and the sobbing ceased.

Natalie's lips curled. Oh yes. Oh hell yes.

What a darkly delicious grin.

ALL SAINTS' DAY

Natalie finished her apple-spiced tea. She sat at Amanda's kitchen table in the morning light.

The house around her bled beauty. Amanda's beauty. The mysterious intensity seeped from every sight and texture. And Amanda's words still lingered from her waking dream.

If we wish hard enough, the cat will come, Amanda said. *We'll be the most powerful witches ever. Rulers of the night. We'll be the dream of every boy. And the envy of every girl.*

Cats are spirits, Natalie said. *Bound to us. Who is going to be ours?*

If I die, I'll be yours, Amanda said. *If you promise to be mine.*

The predator eyes of the cat turned in Natalie's lap.

Delicious hunger now swam, not emptiness.

Natalie heard Nathan's footsteps descending the stairs.

Treats, Tricks, and Terror in Tin Lake

Paula L. Fleming

Adeela carried the candy to the cashier. Six bags. Enough to give every kid in Tin Lake a double fistful. Maybe it would be enough this year.

"Wind sure is picking up out there," said the girl behind the counter. Kristin, Dave Andersen's teenage daughter. She was going away to college next year. She'd never come back except to visit. "It'll be cold for the little ones," Adeela agreed. No matter what the locals really thought of you, most could be counted on to chat about the weather. It was nice, a small blessing in her lonely outpost.

Adeela stepped onto the main street, the wind wrestling her for the door and whipping her full *burka* against her body. A few boys—age twelve or thirteen—circled the deserted intersection. They saw her and their bikes gathered, aligned, as though in a cavalry formation. The tallest boy, blond mullet trying to fly, spearheaded the charge.

Up on the sidewalk they came, bucking their bikes over the curb as though riding in a rodeo, whooping and hollering. Adeela held perfectly still, terrified that any move she made to avoid them would only put her in their path. They swelled, filling her world, their voices impossibly loud and deep with bravado.

"Filthy raghead!"

"Terrorist!"

"Witch!"

And then they were past, hurtling down the street in a fading burst of laughter.

Adeela leaned against the grocery's brick façade and waited for her heart to stop galloping. No matter how much candy she gave out, this would be another horrible Halloween.

She knew the rumors. It was too incredible that a single woman of ultra-conservative Muslim faith would show up in Tin Lake. No one in town really thought she was a Muslim. Instead, the *burka* was thought to hide some terrible deformity. Or she was just crazy, like the people who wore aluminum foil on their heads to keep out the aliens. Ironically, both theories had a kernel of truth. But while the adults were polite as long as she caused no trouble, the children dealt with her strangeness by casting it into molds familiar to them from modern media and ancient folklore. Terrorist. Witch.

Adeela turned the corner and trudged up the hill to the trim Victorian she'd bought in this dying town for less than the price of many cars. She couldn't very well get rid of the *burka*. If the locals didn't like her now . . .

Or could she?

A grin split her thin lips, and her tongue flicked out and touched her nose in amusement. It *was* Halloween. She would answer the door in the nude! The humans would think it was a costume. After all, her kind didn't nurse their young, so she had no breasts to offend anyone. And her hip frill concealed her genitals—they would assume it was a skirt. And if she looked like a proper monster, just the way you were supposed to look on Halloween, maybe the kids would finally give her a break. She wouldn't mind not having to scrape egg off her windows or paint over graffiti this year. She especially wouldn't mind not having a bucket of gasoline balanced on top of her screen door. It had drenched her; the *burka* had been a complete loss, and she hadn't been able to get the smell out of her skin until she went through a molt.

She unlocked the door—she was probably the only resident of Tin Lake who locked her doors—and stepped into the little entryway that preceded the living and dining rooms. She set the bag of candy on the worn oak floor and scooped up the mail from below the slot. Just a circular with ads from the big-box stores in Rim Creek, an hour east, and a bill from the electric co-op.

She went through the arched opening into the dining room and checked her comm unit. Nothing, of course. She wondered, for the thousandth time, if the political situation back home had changed. Had the military taken over? Were cultural xenologists now viewed as traitors for mingling with other species? Had her name and the names of her colleagues at the university been added to the list of undesirables, with a reward for their capture or execution? Were their writings being burned?

Or had money just run short, as it so often did, leaving her department at the short end of the stick again? No money to send a ship to pick her up. And once a line was written out of the budget, it was that much harder to add it back in. She'd drawn up enough grant requisitions herself to know that.

Or maybe it was a change of the political winds. Maybe the military was right now doing recon on earth's defenses—virtually none—and would begin full-scale assault any minute. Earth was a water-rich planet, a prime target for colonization and resource stripping.

It was probably just a budgetary problem. And if the Xenology Department couldn't get the funds from the university, they'd raise them privately. It would just take some time, especially if the southern continent was still in recession. But they wouldn't leave her out here.

Unless there's been a coup.

"Stop it!" She pressed her gloved hands to her temples.

"How can I help you?" asked her system. It always spoke in American-accented English, just in case a human was present.

She wanted to put a fist through its display. But that would be a really bad idea, especially if she was going to be here a lot longer. Her system hacked the amazingly disunified and porous international banking system and siphoned modest sums into her bank account. It had created several ostensible firms that issued her 1099-MISC forms each year, as though she were a contractor for them. Her profession was "consultant." She paid her taxes in full and on time.

"You're very helpful," she told it.

"Thank you."

All right, enough thinking. Without new data, she wouldn't reach any new conclusions. Time for dinner, then to light the pumpkins and wait.

She passed through the kitchen and cast off the cumbersome *burka* before descending the narrow, moldering basement stairs. She hooked her six webbed fingers around the railing to make sure she didn't fall. She could just imagine the scene in the emergency room if she got injured!

The ancient freezer unit kicked on with a moan and a shudder as she opened the door. Frozen fish was gross, but live feeder fish were worse. She wouldn't dare put one of those things in her mouth until she'd treated it with antibiotics for two weeks. And even then, goldfish and guppies . . . yuck.

Back upstairs, she placed the frozen halibut on a baking sheet, spritzed it with lemon juice and drizzled it with olive oil, and stuck it in the oven. While she waited for it to thaw, she grabbed a potato from the frig and bit into it. Potatoes were completely different from anything back home, and awesome. If she ever had a chance to debrief, she'd definitely tell them about potatoes.

And then she concentrated on the crisp, pleasantly musty potato in her mouth and refused to think about her chances of being able to tell her colleagues about it.

On either side of the walkway from sidewalk to porch, the pumpkins grinned or scowled wickedly. Working delicately with a small knife, Adeela had given a few the illusion of having needle teeth like her own. Ten pumpkins. Probably overkill, but she was really trying this year. And she didn't have much else to do.

Naked, thighs modestly pressed together beneath her frill, she sat on the porch steps and watched the jack-o'-lanterns glow brighter as the air dimmed. It was chilly—Adeela felt her circulatory system working harder to pump hot blood from her core out to her hands and feet. The candy was ready beside her in a large plastic "punch bowl." One did not punch it but instead could become punch-drunk drinking spiked (not punched) punch from it. Someday she would have to make punch and drink it out of the bowl to find out what that was about.

A black SUV turned off the main street and rumbled in low gear up the hill. A couple of battered black pickups followed, each with a pair of men in front. As the vehicles climbed past her house, the men looked at her. Well, why not? She was wearing a great Halloween costume!

She waved at them, but they didn't wave back. The trucks took a right at the next block. Hunters? She'd overheard customers discussing pheasant season at the diner. Maybe staying with a friend in town?

A door opened a few houses down, and Cindy Raue emerged with her two little girls. They walked across their lawn to the next house, rang the bell. "Trick-or-treat!" they said in high, delighted voices.

Mom's reminder: "What do you say?"

"Thank you!" in chorus.

Across the next lawn to the next house. Adeela could see them clearly now. The older one was dressed as a "princess," a common figure of children's stories who typically needed rescue. The younger one wore a pillowcase dyed red with black spots. It looked familiar. It was a "ladybug," like those in the summer garden. Ladybugs caught and devoured aphids. Adeela could understand why a child would want to pretend to be a ladybug. She was less certain about the princess fantasy.

Next was Adeela's house. "Oh!" The older girl saw her and stopped dead.

"Do you have candy?" shouted Ladybug, jostling for position.

Last year their mother had ushered them quietly past Adeela's, but Adeela wouldn't give them that choice this time. She stood up with the punch bowl. "Happy Halloween! Such a pretty princess and such a"—she almost said "fierce"—"cute ladybug deserve some treats!"

"It's okay, girls," Cindy Raue said. Adeela gave each a fistful of candy.

"Thank you!" they said.

Ladybug added, "Your costume's cool and scary!"

"I'm glad you like it."

Cindy Raue bit her lower lip and rubbed her hands together nervously, but she looked Adeela in the eyes and said, "That *is* the best costume I have ever seen."

"Thank you, Cindy."

The other woman hesitated a bit more, then said, "Have a nice evening, Adeela."

Hah! A victory. This was working.

The crunch-tinkle of broken glass. Again. And then a boom-whoosh and already the taste of smoke on her sensitive tongue.

Adeela spun around, the punch bowl tumbling down the steps amid a scatter of candy. Inside. Sudden heat. Flames every-where. No, not everywhere. Think! Nothing but smoke yet in the dining room. She needed her system and the comm unit. Everything else she could buy or steal or do without.

She pulled the power unit and adapter, tossed them into a bag, shoved the comm unit in too, broke one of the front windows, and tossed them out on the lawn. The system itself wasn't crash resistant. She wrapped both arms around it and staggered toward the front door, wheezing heavily as smoke filled her lungs.

She reached the little foyer as flames curled around the archway. The ceiling cracked open and a shower of burning wood forced her back.

A window. They'd been painted shut forever ago and were probably stuck. She set the system on the floor, picked up a lamp. Began battering the base against the window, breaking glass and splintering wood. She couldn't breathe. Her arms were growing weak.

Something smashed the glass from the other side. She glimpsed an axe blade through the smoke. Yellow jacket, yellow helmet. A man climbed in, heaved her over his shoulder.

"I need my—," she fumbled for the right human word, "—computer."

And then she floated up and away.

She came to on the front yard across the street. The town fire truck's lights flashed a defiant counterpoint to the flames shooting from her roof. The firefighters were soaking the houses to either side to keep the conflagration from spreading; her home was lost.

More water touched her lips and she grabbed the cup and poured it down. Margaret Saltz, widow of Frank, who'd sold used cars and who owned the lawn she was lying on, took it gently from her and said, "I'll get you some more, dear." Adeela wanted nothing more than a swim in the ocean, but a cup of water was a very good start.

Cindy Raue was there, with the two girls alternately jumping up and down in delight and cowering from the fire.

"Do you want something else to wear?" Cindy asked. "I think we're about the same size."

Adeela thought fast. "Actually, it *is* cold. And the costume is fun but immodest. Do you have anything I could wrap about myself?"

"Oh sure, you gotta wear that Arab thing. I don't . . . Well, it ain't the same thing, but maybe it'd do. My husband's got black plastic tarp in the shed. It won't feel the same as cloth for sure, but it's the look you need, right?"

"That's exactly right. Thank you."

"C'mon girls. That's enough excitement. We're going home." To Adeela, "I'll be right back with the tarp and some scissors. We'll get you dressed proper."

Margaret returned with a pitcher of water. Adeela restrained herself from grabbing it and let Margaret pour her another cup. Old Joe Olson from next door was there, too. She hadn't seen him before. Of course, she hardly saw him in broad daylight when they were both standing in their yards—he had a quiet grayness to him and had never responded to her greetings.

Now he spoke: "Looks like they're gonna save my house, but yours is toast. You gonna need a place to stay."

"Yes, I suppose—"

"You stay with me. I got four bedrooms and the kids are always telling me to move to the city. I get a boarder, it'll shut 'em up. And you always took good care of your roses."

Now one of the firefighters jogged across the street toward her. "Ma'am, just checking. There was no one else in the house, right?"

"No, I live—lived—alone."

"An ambulance is on its way from County, but it's still about 10 minutes out. You okay until then?"

"Thank you, but I won't require medical attention." Adeela made an effort to sit up straight and look like someone who required absolutely no medical attention whatsoever.

"You should be examined…" His radio crackled.

"Were you able to save my computer system? It was on the living room floor when someone carried me out."

"No ma'am. Just you. I gotta get back. Excuse me."

"I'll need a job," Adeela said to no one in particular. She'd felt amazingly normal considering what she'd just been through, but now she was . . . she'd thought of the word earlier . . . punch-drunk. She gulped more water to suppress a giggle.

A couple of sheriff's deputies finished consulting with each other and approached. "You're the homeowner?"

She nodded.

"Did you see anyone unusual before the fire, maybe checking out the place?"

Three vehicles in a row, unsmiling men, not from in town. "Yes." She described them.

They took notes, nodded. "Well we got a couple of 'em. All dressed up in white sheets and everything. Their job was to set a cross on fire in front to take credit for the job. The ones who firebombed the house escaped through the alley, but we've got a pretty good idea where this group bunks down."

Why anyone would want to "take credit" for this, and how setting a cross on fire would do so, and how dressing up as ghosts was related to setting fires, was all a complete mystery. Adeela thought she'd profiled humans pretty thoroughly; clearly she had a lot more research to do. But she just said, "Thank you," and downed another cup of water.

The boys who'd taunted her outside the store rolled up on their bikes to watch the fire. "Awesome!" and "Rad!" they told each other.

She found herself smiling at their sheer innocent enjoyment of a really big fire.

"That's quite a costume." The voice was deep and seemed to crunch over gravel, and it was right in her ear. She jumped up and spun around. It wasn't just the firelight—the man before her wore an outfit of bright red. He was a kind of lobster-devil, with horns and lobster claws and a beaked face and a shell and a long, pointed tail that dragged on the ground behind him. She hoped he wouldn't want to exchange sewing tips—she didn't have any.

"Thank you," she said, for what seemed like the millionth time tonight. Who knew she'd be thanking so many people as her ability to reconnect with her people went up in smoke.

He didn't look at her, or was he glancing slyly her direction out of the corner of his eye? He didn't say anything else, either, but just walked away on giant hooved feet. Now his tail arced up jauntily behind him, its tip twitching.

Bewitched

Shirley Damsgaard

"You can't do this!"

"Wanna bet?" I grabbed a Pyrex dish. "I'm sick of the whole thing...the games, the lies. If Fate isn't going to throw Mr. Right my way, I'll take care of it myself."

"But you don't know what you're doing."

Glancing at my friend Cindy, I could see the disapproval in her eyes. As my appointed "love guru," she had definite ideas on proper dating behavior, and casting a spell on some hapless guy wasn't among them. Not that Joel was hapless...tall, dark hair, dark eyes. I'd been thrilled when he'd singled me out and asked me for a date.

As I traced a finger around the rim of the dish, softness stole over me. Our time together had been magic and I'd felt an immediate connection with him. Suddenly the softness was quashed by the crushing disappointment I'd felt, still felt, when I didn't hear from him again.

Shaking it off, I glared at Cindy. "I do too know," I said, picking up the old, leather book I'd bought at the antique store. "I have this."

To prove my point, I flipped through the pages until I found the right recipe. "See here...'to cleanse your magical space and protect it, first smudge the area with sage. Then take three red candles—'"

Cindy interrupted by closing the cracked cover. "This is nuts. "You can't force someone to fall in love with you. Look, Rachel, he's not worth it. I know you're unhappy—"

"'Unhappy?'" I replied with a snort. "Pissed is more like it." I shoved away from the counter and paced the floor. "'Ooo, baby, those green eyes and that blond hair,'" I said, mimicking Joel's smooth voice. "'Ooo, baby, I can't wait to see you again.'" I stopped and hugged myself tightly. "And like a fool, I believed the lies."

"How many times have I told you, guys tell you what they think you want to hear." She looked up and rolled her eyes. "They're just making conversation."

"Well, it sucks," I cried. "They ought to say what they mean."

"Oh, they do at the time," she said, spreading her hands, "but later..."

"Humph." I marched over to the counter and flung open the book. "This time it's going to be different. This guy's going to get a taste of his own medicine."

"So what are you going to do? Make him fall for you?"

"Yup," I said with a satisfied smile. "Then after I've yanked him around a bit, maybe I'll decide to keep him."

"You don't know anything about this guy. You met him in a bar, for Pete's sake. Even if this hocus-pocus stuff works, how do you know you want a relationship with him? He could be boring."

"He's not. We had fun on our date," I answered defensively.

"One date does not a relationship make." The edge suddenly left her voice. "You're smart. You're funny. There are plenty of guys out there who would be interested. You just haven't found the right one yet."

"I'm tired of looking."

I didn't want to explain how I'd hoped that maybe this time I'd met THE ONE. Explain how those hopes had slowly slid away while I'd made excuses for him not calling after our date.

Maybe he was busy; maybe he was sick; maybe he lost my number. After driving myself crazy for a week, I'd broken Cindy's cardinal rule of *never* calling *them*. Not only had he failed to pick up, he'd never called me back.

I gripped the edge of the counter, staring at the old book. So what the hell? I'd already made the mistake of contacting him. What could one little spell hurt now?

With a shake of her head, she shrugged. "I give up." Grabbing her purse, she strode to the kitchen door, then stopped. "If you don't blow yourself up or get carried off by demons, you're still coming to the Halloween party tomorrow night, aren't you?"

"You bet," I answered with a big smile. "Wait until you see my costume…Dorothy. I even have ruby slippers."

A bark of laughter rang out. "Well, if anyone ever believed in fantasy, it's you!" Her eyes traveled back to the book. "Just don't change your mind and come as a witch, okay?"

After Cindy left, I hustled around, organizing my supplies. Sage? Nope, but I did have oregano. Close enough. Rose oil to anoint the candles? Gosh, didn't have any of that either, but I did have some very expensive Este Lauder bath oil. Oil's oil, right? Paper and a pen to write down my heart's desire? Not a problem.

Once everything was laid out on the counter, I dumped half a jar of dried oregano leaves into the Pyrex dish. Taking a match, I lit it and dropped it onto the oregano. Soon my entire kitchen smelled like a pizza parlor.

Glancing at the book again, I poured a large amount of the bath oil into my palms. Some of it ran across the counter; I grabbed a paper towel and wiped up the spill. Tossing the towel aside, I anointed the three red candles. Next step: carve Joel's name three times on each candle.

Finished, I moved on to my heart's desire. I paused and stared down at the blank paper while a chill crept up my arms. Did I really want to do this? Was Cindy right? How much did I know about Joel? On our date, he'd been charming and attentive. But was that enough? Now that I thought about it, he'd been a little hesitant in talking about himself.

"No," said a voice in my head. "He made you feel special. Don't you want to feel that way again?"

"Yes," I whispered.

After lighting the candles, I let all my hopes and dreams for true love pour onto the paper. Finished, I folded it nine times and place it on top of the still smoking oregano. Lighting another match, I touched it to the folded paper.

It flared and black smoke began to roll out of the bowl. *Way too much smoke.* My eyes watered. Grabbing at the bowl, I tried to set it in the sink, but the Pyrex was too hot. My hand jerked and hit the third candle. It fell onto the oil-soaked paper towel, catching *it* on fire. The smoke thickened and suddenly the silence of the kitchen was broken by a shrill sound.

"Way to go," I choked as smoke clogged my mouth. "You've set off the smoke detectors."

I didn't have time to worry about the alarm. The fire had begun to snake its way across the counter. Grabbing the sprayer, I dowsed the flames until my attempt at magic was nothing more than a sodden mess.

I turned to run down the hall and shut off the smoke detector. Before I could take a step, a loud rap sounded at my back door, followed by the voice of my elderly neighbor, Miss Eva.

"Rachel! What's going on?"

"Just a minute, Miss Eva," I yelled.

I hurried down the hall, and, grabbing a chair, pulled it toward the deafening sound. Climbing, I yanked off the detector cover. The smoke was thicker near the ceiling and it burned my lungs. Holding my breath, I tore the battery out. Sweet silence.

Jumping off the chair, I ran to the kitchen and flung open the door. Miss Eva stood on the back step with a look of concern on her face.

"Lordy, child, what's going on?" she asked, clutching the

frayed edges of her battered robe. "You've soot on your face." She leaned to the side, trying to peer around me.

I sidestepped, blocking her view. "Oh, umm, well…" My voice trailed away as I tried to think of a logical explanation. I didn't dare tell this sweet lady about my aborted attempt at spell casting. "A small fire. Ah, I was cooking…yeah, that's it." The lie tumbled out of my mouth. "I was frying bacon and the grease caught fire."

"Goodness, you're lucky you didn't burn your house down."

No kidding. Wait a second—our houses were so far apart—"Miss Eva, how—?"

"I heard that alarm of yours," she said, cutting off my question.

"Really?" I glanced at the house across the alley. Did the smoke detector wake up anyone else? Miss Eva did have the habit of wandering around her yard at night. She claimed it was the best time to water her huge garden. The other neighbors thought her actions weird, but I'd chalked it up to poor sleep patterns and boredom. What *does* a little old woman do at three o'clock in the morning? Watch the Home Shopping Network? Miss Eva wasn't the type.

Miss Eva tugged on my arm. "Don't worry, dear, I'm the only one who heard it."

She offered to stay and help me clean up the mess, but I assured her that everything was fine and finally got her to leave. Then I turned to survey my kitchen.

Mess was an understatement. Flakes of charred paper towel littered the counter; red wax from the overturned candles had hardened on the scorched Formica; and puddles of water glistened across the kitchen linoleum. Throwing my hands in the air, I shook my head.

Some witch I'd make. I should've listened to Cindy…not only was it wrong to try and force Joel to love me, but I'd almost lost my house in the process. Was the Universe trying to tell me something?

With a chagrined smile, I turned my back on the disaster and went to bed.

❖

Fresh paint and stain block for my kitchen walls and ceiling—seventy bucks. Purchasing and installing a new section of counter top—seven hundred and fifty. The lesson I learned—priceless. I was done with magic and done with men. If Mr. Right was out there, he was going to have to find me.

"Now this," I muttered as my stilettos clicked on the sidewalk in front of the bar holding the Halloween party. I'd been so busy running around lining up the repairs to my kitchen that I hadn't checked on my "Dorothy" costume. The costume company had screwed up and given me the wrong size. It hugged curves that I didn't even know I had. I'd also had to replace the size-six ruby slippers with my size-eight red stilettos. If Dorothy had worn shoes like these, she'd never have made it to the Emerald City.

After opening the door, I paused for a moment as my eyes adjusted to the dim light. The room was full of witches, vampires, and various other monsters. Finally I spied my friends sitting at a table on the far side of the room. Pushing past the revelers, I toddled over to them.

They were all in the spirit of Halloween. Cheryl was dressed as Raggedy Ann, June was a "biker babe", and Cindy was a sexy witch. Eyeing her costume, I raised a brow.

"I thought you said no 'witches'?"

"I wanted you to feel at home," she said with a sly grin.

"Funny," I shot back, pulling out a chair and taking my seat.

I ordered a beer, but before I could take a single sip I felt a hand on my shoulder. Looking up, I saw the handsomest vampire in the room hovering over me. Joel.

Cindy, quickly taking in the situation, nudged both Cheryl and June. "Let's go dance."

In a second, they were lost in the mass of bodies on the

crowded dance floor, leaving me alone with Joel.

"Mind if I sit down?" He motioned toward Cindy's vacant chair.

My tongue seemed to be stuck to the roof of my mouth and all I could do was shake my head 'no.'

Once seated, he leaned in close. "I'm sorry I didn't call you." Placing his hand on the table, he stared at me intently and I found myself being pulled in by his dark brown eyes. "Right after our date I had to go out of town. By the time I got back I was afraid it was too late and that you'd be angry." He traced a line across the table toward my hand. "Are you angry?"

Watching Joel and hearing his smooth voice, I once again felt the attraction weave its way around me and into my heart. Every ounce of his being was focused on me. I stared back at him, hypnotized. The crowd and the noise faded until it seemed we were the only two people in the room.

"N-n-no," I stammered. "But I called you, and left messages."

"You did? I never received them." He leaned forward. "Believe me, Rachel, if I would've known you weren't angry I'd have called you back."

He sounded so sincere. Did I dare believe him?

A grin spread across his face as he took in my costume. "You look gorgeous tonight. I love a woman in red stilettos," he whispered and laid his hand on top of mine. Slowly he stroked his thumb across my fingers.

Dropping my chin, I stared as his thumb traced a lazy pattern over each knuckle. Shivering, I raised my eyes and saw him, really saw him.

Reality slammed into me. His eyes weren't warm and his smile was almost feral. I yanked my hand away and dropped it onto my lap as I thought about the hell I put myself through waiting for his call; the desperation that had driven me to attempt magic. Did I want someone who might be manipulated by a spell? Someone who spouted honeyed words as intangible as the smoke that had filled my kitchen?

No!

Leaning back in my chair, I crossed my arms over the too-tight bodice. "Look Joel, I appreciate your explanation, but you know...I just don't think we're a good match."

"What do you mean?" he asked in a shocked voice. "I thought we'd connected."

"I did have fun, but I don't think we're right for each other..." I paused. "But I hope we can be friends."

A look of anger crossed his face before his charming mask fell into place. Reaching across the table, he laid his arm on the back of my chair, and as he did, his cologne—a scent that had haunted me for the past week—assaulted my senses. My stomach clenched.

Edging back, I tried to escape the cloying smell. "Joel, you're a nice guy, but it won't work," I said quickly. "I hope you find what you're looking for."

His eyes traveled down to the floor. "I thought I did."

"Sorry."

Joel raised his head and focused his attention on a spot over my right shoulder, cutting off my words. I turned to see Cindy, June, and Cheryl standing in a half-circle around the back of my chair. June placed a protective hand on my shoulder and stared pointedly at Joel.

He got the hint. "Ladies," he said with a tight smile and a slight bow. Moments later he was across the room, chatting up another blonde.

❖

Later that night I plopped down on my bed and, kicking off my shoes, let my toes curl in relief at their sudden freedom. Lying back, I stared at the ceiling and thought about my evening. I'd had fun—a lot of fun. It was great laughing and dancing with my friends, not obsessing over some guy. Lightness settled in my heart, and I jumped up, sashaying across the room as I threw on my robe. In the bathroom, I hummed to myself while

I squirted a drop of cleanser in my hand. The past week I'd been so focused on Joel that I'd forgotten about me, forgotten all the positive things in my life. My job, my family, my friends. Even without Mr. Right, life was pretty good.

I'd just slathered my face with the cleanser when I heard it—a soft snick, like a window quietly closing. I paused and shut off the water as I listened. Nope—nothing. Turning the faucet back on, I closed my eyes and scrubbed. Finished, I groped for the towel and dried off my face. When I dropped it, the smell hit me and my eyes flew open.

Joel stood leaning against the bathroom door.

Whirling, I stumbled back against the counter. "What are you doing here? How did you get in?"

He held up his hands and smiled. "Calm down. I just want to talk to you. We could've settled this at the bar, but your friends interrupted us."

"There's nothing to settle," I said, keeping my voice even. "Please leave."

He shoved away from the door. "Come on, baby, you don't mean that. You want me. You know you do. You left me all those voice messages."

So he'd lied to me about that, too. Anger battled with my fear. Who did this guy think he was? Sneaking into my house?

"This is crazy," I muttered.

His eyes flared wide. "Don't say that!" he exclaimed. "I'm not crazy."

"Joel, I didn't mean—"

Pacing back and forth in the doorway, his lips twisted into an ugly sneer. "I don't know how many times I have to say it before someone understands. I thought you understood," he said, jabbing a finger in my direction. "You wore those red shoes tonight. Shoes so shiny and bright..."

As I listened to him ramble on about my shoes, terror replaced my anger. This guy *was* crazy! *I'm trapped in my bathroom with a crazy man!*

The window. If I could reach it I'd throw it open and scream. Maybe it would scare him enough to leave. I took one cautious step sideways and my fingers grazed against my can of hairspray. At the same time, Joel stopped his ranting and turned his attention to me.

"You're just like the others," he said sadly, moving to close the distance between us.

Too late for the window. Grabbing the hairspray, I waited until he was right in front of me. Then I sprayed.

He shrieked as it hit him square in the eyes. Stumbling, he fell against the wall and I darted past him, heading for the stairs and the front door. When I reached the stairs, my robe whipped around my ankles and I came close to tumbling. Grabbing the banister, I righted myself and kept moving. Steps thundered behind me.

"Oh my god," I gasped, "I'm not going to make it."

I ran faster.

At the door, I grabbed the knob and yanked. The door opened and I stumbled into the night…and the arms of a cop.

Relief buckled my knees. "He's—he's—"

The cop shoved me behind him and drew his gun. Quickly he called for backup, and seconds later sirens wailed. In a blur, I was hustled into a waiting patrol car while police poured out of their vehicles and into my house. Soon two officers were leading a handcuffed Joel out the door and into another car. A moment later it roared away.

A tap on the window drew my attention. My rescuer stood waiting outside the door. I opened it and he crouched down.

"Are you okay?"

I nodded, noticing the two plastic bags he held in one hand. One contained a roll of duct tape, a strand of rope, and a knife. The other held my red shoes.

"Wh—what's that?" I asked.

The cop hesitated. "It's called a kill kit. You were lucky your neighbor called and reported a prowler."

"He's a killer?" I asked stunned.

"Based on this," he said, his grip tightening on the two bags, "we believe he's the Red Shoe Killer. Don't worry, he's going away for a long time." Standing, he held out his hand.

Grabbing it like a lifeline, I rose on wobbly legs.

"We'll need a statement from you, but it can wait. Is there somewhere you can stay tonight?"

I took a deep breath. "I'll call one of my fr—"

"Nonsense," said an elderly voice, cutting me off.

Miss Eva, dressed in her ratty robe, pushed past the cop and threw an arm around my shoulders. "You'll stay with me. I'll bring her to the station in the morning," she said with a nod.

Walking across the yard with Miss Eva, I finally felt safe. "I can never thank you enough... I—"

She dismissed my expressions of gratitude with a wave. "I'm glad I could help. But Rachel, this late night excitement at your house does need to stop and I have just the thing that will help. A lovely potted geranium." Leaning in close, she whispered in my ear, "When it comes to protection, geraniums work so much better than oregano."

The Replacement

Anne Frasier

Eighteen-year-old Grant Vang shot around the corner on his ten-speed, hopped the curb, then veered sharply to miss a group of university students clustered on the sidewalk.

Frat boys. Dinkytown was famous for frat boys and Bob Dylan. And more recently, the University of Minnesota student who'd been killed in a hazing.

"Watch it, freak!" one of the cluster shouted.

Without looking, Grant threw them the finger. He turned into a narrow alley, jumped off the bike, and ran beside it before stopping. A quick lock, then he stepped into his uncle's shop.

The old man spoke from a dark corner. "You're late."

Grant waited for his eyes to adjust. The scent of unburned incense barely covered the sweet-sour stench of decay. "I've been busy."

"Have you found someone to take your place?"

"I'm working on it."

"You have to get a replacement. You don't have much time left."

"Replacements aren't that easy to come by."

His uncle made a clicking sound with his tongue. "You're too picky."

155

"I can't use just anybody."

"One human is as good as another."

"No." His uncle was always talking about children. No children. Grant wouldn't use children.

The bell above the door rang, announcing a customer.

The university student. The one Grant had almost hit.

He glanced at Grant, then strolled to a shelf and feigned interest in the jars and candles. He picked up a carved wooden box. "What's this?"

"A reanimation kit."

The kid made a ho-ho-ho face. "To bring somebody back to life? People pay you for this crap? Looks like it's been opened. Like it's been used."

"Nothing here is new."

"You sell old stuff? What kind of place is this?"

"My uncle is a doctor."

The kid snorted. "Whatever you say."

Grant heard his uncle humming behind him. Even though Grant didn't turn around, he knew the old man's eyes would be closed, his hands folded on the top of his cane.

The hum? "Sign on the Window." Sometimes it was "Lay Lady Lay," but he tended to go with Dylan's more obscure work. Occasionally he'd toss in a Springsteen number.

"You tell him what's wrong and he puts together ingredients that will cure you," Grant said. "He can cure anything. Got STDs? If you do, he can get rid of them."

"Hey, man. I'm clean."

"He can also create a spell that will bring about your heart's desire."

"Yeah, right."

"Money. Love. Fame. A truckload of beer. Whatever you want." Grant took the wooden box and replaced it on the shelf.

Now that they stood face to face, the frat boy's eyes narrowed. "You look familiar. Have we met before? I mean before you almost ran over me out there."

"We all look alike, don't we?"

The visitor shrugged. "What are you? Japanese?"

"Try Hmong." But Grant had looked in the mirror and knew he'd indeed changed.

The old man jotted something down on a piece of paper, his pen scratching like a knife. The paper was folded three times and handed to Grant. Grant passed it on.

"Jesus Christ," the kid said. "Your fingers are like ice. And your skin... If your uncle's so great, why doesn't he do something about *that*?"

"I try, but the boy doesn't listen," the old man said.

Grant felt his cheek. Peeling. "It just started." His uncle was right; he didn't have much time left.

The kid held up the paper. "What's this?"

"Memorize the words, then eat them. After the sun sets below the horizon and the moon is a sliver in the night sky, stand with your back to the foot of a fresh grave, close your eyes, and repeat what it says three times." Grant held out his hand. "Twenty bucks."

"Twenty bucks? For some words on a piece of paper?"

"That's cheap for your heart's desire, wouldn't you say?"

"I'm not paying you a dime. Here are some words: Fuck you."

"Go alone," Grant told him. "You have to go alone or it won't work."

The kid turned and left. Grant turned to his uncle and they smiled in wordless communication.

❖

The frat boy's heels sank into the soft dirt. He closed his eyes and repeated the words from the paper. Bob Dylan lyrics. Grant almost laughed out loud when he heard them, because of course the words weren't important. They were just a means to an end.

It had been a gamble. Grant hadn't been sure the kid would come, but he'd heard that killers often visited their victims' graves, and this was one of the few fresh burials in the area.

Now he stepped out from behind a tree trunk, put his hand to the young man's chest, and shoved. The guy crashed through the grave blanket of woven fronds and funeral flowers to the open coffin below.

Grant slammed the lid on the box, then began shoveling while the kid screamed and pounded. The dirt was soft, and it didn't take long. Soon Grant was patting the soil into a smooth mound. He ran his fingers across the headstone.

GRANT VANG.

If anybody were to ask how it felt to be dead, he'd have to say pretty damn nasty. He'd been pissed when his uncle had used the reanimation kit on him because it had meant the possibility of days of pain and agony before dying all over again. Reanimated bodies only lasted so long without a replacement—that was how those things worked.

When he got home to the apartment next to the shop, he kicked off shoes covered in grave dirt and plopped into a chair.

"Done?" his uncle asked, offering him a bowl of popcorn.

"Done." Grant shook his head, queasy at the thought of testing his teeth and digestive system so soon.

"I don't know why you're so reluctant to use a child to fill your empty grave. A child would have bought you more time."

"No children."

His uncle shrugged. It was something they would never agree on. "What does it matter? We are all reborn." He claimed to have lived twenty-eight lives. "Is it so wrong that I want you to fall in love? Experience life? See the world beyond Dinkytown?"

Grant thought about the girl he might meet, and the kids he might have.

Settling in for the night, the old man picked up the remote control and turned on the news.

A reporter stood near an iron gate, microphone in hand. "A

cell-phone call from a grave led police to a local cemetery and a suspected prank," the woman said. "But instead they arrived to discover the body of the university student allegedly involved in the hazing death of Grant Vang earlier this week. Odder still, Vang's body was no longer in the grave."

"What goes around comes around," the old man said with a mouthful of popcorn.

"His cell phone." Grant examined his hands. The skin was young and healthy again. He would live. For how long, nobody knew. A year. Maybe ten. There were no absolutes in reanimation. "Never thought about his cell phone."

"It takes practice to get these things right. Next time you'll know."

Practice. Grant hated to think of having to go through this again.

Someone knocked and Grant answered the door.

"Trick-or-treat!" On the front step stood a zombie accompanied by two small vampires.

"Where's your costume?" one of the vampires asked in the excited way of kids on a sugar high. "You should have a costume!"

"Not now." Grant grabbed a sack of candy bars and tore open one end. "It feels good to look normal." He dropped a treat in each paper bag. "I've been dead three days."

They screamed in delight and pretend terror. Then, in a swirl of tattered fabric and fake blood, they ran to the next porch light.

This Old House

Paul D. Brazill

Ten Sycamore Hill was, in Peter Ord's mind, the font of all of his misfortunes. While women, work, cars and kids came and went, the only constant in Peter's turbulent life—apart from the copious amounts of alcohol he consumed—was the weather-beaten Victorian overlooking Hart Village, its increasingly battered facade and interior seeming to degenerate with each one of his trials and tribulations.

With every one of Peter's disappointments, a window frame would crumble. With every disaster, romantic or otherwise, a door handle would come loose or slates would be ripped from the roof by an unsympathetic wind. When his health failed, so did the heating. And, as Peter's bank account dwindled, the wallpaper and paint seemed to peel free from the walls before his eyes.

Each night, as a drunken Peter staggered back from another interminable drinking session at the Raby Arms, he would look up at his home perched on the hill, looming over the village like a great black crow and, soaked in alcoholic self-pity, he would curse: "Fuck."

Or words to that effect.

And then one late October night, Peter had an idea so bright that it was positively incandescent.

❖

The Raby Arms, an anonymous country pub amongst a cluster of anonymous country pubs, was always smoggy despite the smoking ban. And, indeed, the interior, including the mirrors, the windows and the faces of most of the regulars, all seemed to have a nicotine sheen. As on most nights, Peter found the pub half empty.

J.T., a gaunt, jaundiced-looking man with a spidery black quiff, sat at his usual corner table near a buzzing slot machine, drumming his fingers on his pint glass to The Shadow's "Apache," which played from a crackly speaker.

"You know, it's actually possible to kill someone with a bottle of Pepsi and a packet of Mentos?" said J.T., peeling an unlit pin-sized roll up from his bottom lip.

"Oh, aye?" Peter hung his camel coat on the moose-head rack and sat opposite J.T. with a sigh. "Not a lot of people know that."

"Aye," said J.T. "Well, according to your good friend Big Jim, that is. He reckons that he saw it on YouTube."

Peter sipped his pint of Stella, gazed at the fading bat-wing tattoos on his hands, and faded in on the memory of a drunken night at a Newcastle tattoo parlor that then segued into the time he first met his wife, Deborah, at Astros nightclub. Twenty-five years ago now. There'd been a lot of booze under the bridge since then.

He looked at J.T., a former hard man just like him, and had a flashback to the night when it all started to go wrong. When they'd thrown a rowdy punter down the stairs at Astros with a little too much enthusiasm. The policemen on the scene had also shown a little too much enthusiasm for the arrest, and the ensuing injuries had, luckily for them, resulted in a suspended sentence.

Peter's thoughts were interrupted by a loud bang, and then Big Jim burst through the doors. Peter and J.T. both laughed as Jim stumbled into the toilets, his fly open, muttering to himself.

J.T. shook his head. "You're still going ahead with it?"

Peter shrugged and winced with pain. 'So you reckon it's a non-starter then?' he said, massaging his left arm.

J.T. took a swig of Stella.

"Oh, aye. Great idea. Get Big Jim—Big Jim of all people—to burn down your house on Bonfire Night and then collect on the insurance. A foolproof plan, that. About as foolproof as that canoeist that did a Lord Lucan and ended up getting spotted in Rio or somewhere."

J.T. had a point, thought Peter. Big Jim wasn't exactly the sharpest tool in the box. However, Jim was cheap and Peter really wanted rid of that house. The bills were mounting up and the Invalidity Benefit that he's started getting after his first heart attack barely covered his drinking sessions.

Peter sighed again and slouched in his chair as he wiped his sweating brow with his tie. "It's Guy Fawkes night in less than a week," he said. "Kids are always pushing bangers and fireworks through people's letterboxes. The firemen will be run off their feet. Now, if I happen to leave some booze splashed around the place and work on my motorbike in the front room and it catches fire, well..."

They both looked up as Big Jim plonked himself down next to them.

"Peter, I'm your man," said Big Jim.

"Oh, I'll take that with a mountain of Saxa," said J.T.

❖

Halloween found Peter propped up at the bar tearing the label from a bottle of Newcastle Brown, watching *Deal Or No Deal* while trying to ignore the numb feeling in his arm. It had been creeping up on him with greater regularity these days. Doctors were out of the question. Overpaid quacks. A conviction that had been reinforced when Dr. Kay misdiagnosed his dad's cancer a few years back. Feeling weak, he headed for a battered armchair in the corner. And then he heard the explosion.

"Bollocks! He hasn't…He – "

Hot, sweating and wheezing, Peter rushed out of the pub and up the cobbled path towards his burning home. "Tosser!" he shouted at Big Jim, who tripped, tumbled and stumbled down the path in a panic.

As the pain in his arm got worse, Peter heard a sound behind him, turned and saw a small group of vampires, werewolves and ghosts waving pumpkins.

"Trick-or-treat!" they shouted as they approached.

"Oh, bollocks," Peter gasped, as he crumpled to the ground like a demolished building. The idiot had confused Halloween with Guy Fawkes Night.

The weight of a mammoth was on Peter's chest before the last stages of the coronary kicked in. While he writhed in pain, the costumed kids deftly lifted his wallet and watch. As his vision began to fade like hot breath on a cold windowpane, Peter looked up at his burning house silhouetted against the waxing moon. He could see the front door glowing red like the eyes and mouth of a grinning Jack o'-lantern, the flames darting like a maniac's tongue.

And then, melding with the screams of the approaching fire engines, Peter thought he heard a mocking laugh.

BOO!

Michael Allan Mallory

Leonard Skupic lay in wait for his next victim, barely able to contain himself. It wouldn't be long. He had a great view of the front walk. And he could bide his time. With the electric lights out, no one was likely to see him at the window; the six jar candles on the fireplace mantel offered little in the way of illumination. Mood lighting. Even if anyone did notice his head and shoulders in the living room window, they'd be hard pressed to make out his shape within the ambiguous confluence of light and shadow.

Approaching laughter caught his ear. Four small figures emerged from the tar-colored darkness. Leonard crouched lower, his fingers squeezing the two cords passing through the partly open window sash. One cord was tied to the wicker chair, the other went to Joe Scarecrow, a life-sized stuffed cloth dummy dressed in a flannel shirt, patched coveralls and hat. Yellow straw hair poked out from under the floppy hat. Black button eyes and a garish grin leered malevolently.

Leonard wore the same grin.

A pirate, a witch, a zombie, and a super hero climbed the three creaky wooden steps to the porch. Under the amber glow of the overhead porch light, they paused before the red door to boost their courage.

The pirate reached out to push the doorbell. Leonard drew in a breath—and tugged the first cord. The wicker chair scritched back on the floorboards.

Four little heads turned in unison.

Leonard yanked the second cord. Joe Scarecrow flew out of the chair at the children.

"Eeee!" cried the witch.

The zombie, smallest of the candy crew, backed away with concern.

"It's fake, Bobby," the pirate told him. "It's not real."

The zombie looked unconvinced.

Laughing, Leonard hoisted himself up and rushed to the door. "Boo!" he said, holding out a large ceramic bowl brimming with candy treats that instantly reminded the youngsters of their purpose.

"Trick-or-treat!" Four cloth bags were thrust out.

Leonard dropped handfuls of mini candy bars and suckers into each bag.

"Thank you," said a chorus of happy voices.

He watched the children trundle back down the path into the night, inspecting their bags, taking stock of their loot. Leonard collected Joe Scarecrow and reset the trap. A smile of nostalgia came to him as he adjusted the dummy. The raggedy coveralls had been his a lifetime ago, the first year he and Molly had lived in the old bungalow. Leonard had ripped the pants while repairing the rain gutters. The pillowcase head was Molly's handiwork, cut, sewn and painted by her.

With Joe Scarecrow back in his chair, Leonard went inside and took up his post by the window, patient as a basement spider. He didn't spring the trap on every caller. Sometimes they came too quickly. Other times he simply preferred waiting for the 'right' victim. That was the fun. Once a year Halloween gave him an excuse to play pranks. Decorating the house had always been Molly's task, one she loved. Halloween was her absolute favorite holiday. Over the years they'd seen fewer and fewer trick-or-treaters. A sign of the times, he knew. Most kids now-adays spent the holiday at the mall or in a private home for safety. Guess there were too many real weirdos out there now, not just the pretend crazies.

A noise.

Leonard squinted into the darkness. The sound came from near the boulevard hackberry whose yellow leaves shuddered in the wind. Deformed shadows materialized by the tree trunk to congeal into the shape of three teenagers. Their loud voices carried from the sidewalk.

Oh, yes, they would do very well.

Out of habit, Leonard glanced behind at Molly's empty wing chair, as if expecting her to be seated there with her crossword puzzles, gazing back with a contented smile. Only she wasn't there. His face dimmed at how empty the chair was without her, at how silent the house was without her laughter. Eighteen months. Leonard sighed. It was still a struggle for him. The last Halloween had been rough. Too many memories. Too soon after her death. Even the thought of putting up decorations had been unbearable.

In time the hurt had dulled, though it continued to nibble away at him like the arthritis in his knee. It wasn't until August that he'd finally summoned up the will to clean out her things, which is when he came across the Halloween boxes under the basement stairs. Molly's boxes. He hadn't the heart to throw them out. After a week he decided, on a whim, to put out one little witch figurine, the first decoration he'd bought for her. It was only supposed to be up for a couple of days but was soon joined by a plastic Frankenstein doll which Molly had agonized over buying. The two objects were a comfort in an odd way, giving him the illusion she'd just put them out herself and would return shortly. As September faded into October, skulls and rubber dismembered hands emerged from the boxes to be followed by cotton cobwebs, plastic bats, black and orange crepe paper, and other ghoulish iconography.

She'd approve, Leonard thought, looking around. While he didn't possess Molly's decorating sense, he felt the effort wasn't half bad—

Leonard's ears pricked. The voices were close now. A goth teenaged girl was in front. Black hair, black eye makeup, black lipstick, black clothes. The girl next to her was also a young teen, this one in a Kool-Aid red mohawk, candy red lipstick, and facial piercings. Their companion was a pale male vampire. Too old to spook? Worth a try, Leonard thought. The moment they stepped onto the porch he yanked the cords. The wicker-chair legs scuttled back and Joe Scarecrow flew out.

"Shit!" Goth Girl jumped.

"It's fake, you dumbass." Mohawk Girl nudged the fallen dummy with the toe of her army boot.

Vampire Teen was too cool to impress beyond a simple raised eyebrow. "Lame," he said.

The red door flew open.

"BOO!" Leonard stood large in the doorframe. His welcoming grin evaporated as he saw the bored expressions on the teenager's faces. Apparently, he was unworthy of even a holiday salutation. The vampire thrust out a canvas bag. "Trick-or-treat, man."

Leonard knit his brow in disapproval. "Aren't you a little old to be out asking for candy, son?"

The vampire snorted. "We'll take cash."

"Hmmpf. I don't like that."

Mohawk Girl cut in and jiggled her loot bag. "You gonna give us candy or not?"

For an instant the temptation to say no played on his lips; however, before the words came out he heard the echo of Molly's sweet chiding voice in his mind. "Oh, Leonard, lighten up. What are a few pieces of candy? You can keep the spirit of the day even if they can't." And he wanted to honor her memory. Retrieving the candy bowl, he loaded their bags and tried to show he wasn't such an old grump. "I like your costumes."

Goth Girl squinted. "Costumes?"

Leonard gestured at their clothes.

"We aren't wearing costumes!" Mohawk Girl shot him a baleful look and wheeled about in a huff. She clomped down the steps, followed by her friends.

Speechless, Leonard watched them laugh derisively as they walked away.

Oh well…

He set Joe Scarecrow in the wicker chair and returned to the window, though he didn't know why he bothered. The mood was broken. What was the point? It was all a sham. It was a mistake thinking he could do this without Molly.

A small ceramic werewolf stared at him from the window-sill. Leonard took it, caressing its smooth surface. Molly's first effort in her ceramics class, before she got good.

The accident happened on her way to class. A drunk driver had run her down, a five-time offender who wasn't supposed to be on the road. Some irresponsible punk who figured the law didn't apply to him! The anger welled up inside Leonard like a suppressed scream. He hurled the figurine across the room where it smashed to pieces against the floor. Eyes jammed shut, he tried to block out the memory of that awful night.

It was a while before Leonard dared to open his eyes. When he did, he saw a ghostly reflection of his face in the window, a grim and hollow-eyed countenance as devoid of life as the plastic monsters around him. Was this his life now? In their kinder moments, his friends suggested he should move on, deal with life after Molly, though that had proven to be more difficult than he'd expected.

A swirl of wind scratched a pile of dead leaves along the sidewalk. The noise drew his attention. Someone else was coming up the walk. No kid, it was an adult draped in a dark, hooded robe. A bony hand held a tall scythe. The trick-or-treater was dressed like Death.

Now this was too much! The adult candy moocher was the

last straw. Leonard jumped up and flung open the front door. "Do you know how ridiculous you look? I'm sick and tired of you adults begging for treats. Buy your own damned candy!" Leonard tried to look his caller in the eye but couldn't see the other's face inside the dark hood. The overhead porch light cast a heavy shadow.

"Leonard Skupic," Death intoned in a deliberate, resonant voice, "I have come for you."

"I get it, you're really into the part. Now take a hike before I slam the door in your face."

"I am Death, Leonard Skupic, you will come with me."

"Now you're getting tiresome."

Silence.

Leonard sighed. "Maybe you think this is funny. Look, I'm in a crappy mood and don't feel like playing your game. Just go."

Death stood his ground.

"Cripes!" Leonard threw up his hands. "Don't you understand English? I said I'm not interested in playing your stupid game. Get off my property!" Stepping back, Leonard slammed shut the big red door and shook his head. Some people!

When he got back to the window, he was surprised to see the visitor had not moved. "This guy's really starting to annoy me," he grumbled, just about ready to close the curtains when Death turned about and glided down the path. Too curious to look away, Leonard wondered where he'd go next. The Carlsons? Good luck with that! Loren Carlson would probably invite him in for a beer and talk his ear off. Yet instead of taking a right at the sidewalk, Death went left and faded into the evening somewhere behind Joe Scarecrow's head. Leonard leaned to the side for a better look.

A twitch.

Joe Scarecrow suddenly sat bolt upright. His head snapped round to stare malignantly at Leonard. "BOO!" he shouted, then lunged at the window with both arms extended.

Leonard recoiled, nearly swallowing his heart. Braced for an attack, he was surprised when it didn't come. The window was still intact. Joe Scarecrow still lay limp in his chair like the collection of old clothes and rags he was. Leonard eyed him warily and gulped in calming breaths.

Deep calming breaths—

He stopped.

Leonard realized he was not alone.

From the corner of his eye he saw it, the flutter of a black robe. He turned, dreading what he'd see, but knowing there was no way he could avoid looking. Death stood there like a dark angel, his scythe held out before him. "Leonard Skupic," he spoke, "I have come for you."

Leonard swallowed.

Death took a step closer. "Do you believe me this time?"

"Y-yes. Um, sorry about before. I didn't know it was really you."

As if in acknowledgement, Death inclined his head. In the dim candlelight, Leonard still could not see the hooded face, yet he felt the eyes inside the black void staring directly into his soul.

"Does this mean I'm dead?" Leonard brought a hand to his face. "I don't feel dead."

"You are still among the living, Leonard Skupic, until I take you away."

"This must be a mistake!"

"I do not make mistakes."

Leonard nodded. "I suppose I can't change your mind."

A heavy silence.

The hooded figure offered no clemency. With no court of appeal open to him, Leonard felt his mortality closing around him. He bowed his head in acquiescence. After a moment, he looked up. "Um, will Molly be there? Be where you're taking me?"

"Yes."

"Will I see her?"

"You will."

The promise eased his anxiety. "Am I supposed to go with you now?"

For several seconds Death did not speak. When he stirred, it was to lower himself into Molly's wing chair where he made himself comfortable. He set his scythe against the wall and folded his hands in his lap. "We have time yet. I have traveled far and you are my last call."

Laughter from outside.

Leonard looked through the window and scowled. "It's those goth teenagers again. Hey, that's my planter! Did you see that? They just knocked it over. They're coming back to the house." He shook his head. "No respect...and I gave them candy." Leonard glared at Death. "Damn, I'd really like to teach them a lesson."

"What kind of lesson?"

"I don't know, something to shake them up, something to scare 'em into realizing their actions have consequences."

After pondering this for a bit, Death leaned forward in Molly's chair. "Scare them...I think I can help you with that."

Leonard looked back, intrigued. "Oh, this is going to be good."

Girls from the North Country

Theresa Weir

I moved to the middle of nowhere to get away from people. To reach my cabin in the north woods of Minnesota, a person has to drive miles on a rutty road that washes out in heavy rain. When the road finally stops, that same person must hike another three miles. In winter, nobody can get in or out and that suits me just fine.

In summer, I get strays. City boys turned nature boys who show up on the front porch wearing a backpack and shaggy beard. They left civilization for an adventure in the wilderness, but five days in they spot my cabin and run straight for it, unable to tolerate their own company any longer.

"How do you stand it out here by yourself?" they always ask. "How do you keep from losing your mind?"

"I don't," I tell them. And then I smile, giving them that hatchet-man leer. Well, hatchet-female. They smile back, but the return smile is awkward and fake and wobbly. Because yes, a person has to be a bit crazy to embrace complete isolation.

I have everything I need. A little woodstove that keeps me warm. A stockpile of supplies carted in when the roads and trails are passable. All I ask from the world is to be left alone.

Just me, myself, and I.

My days are plenty busy, what with chopping and carrying wood, and melting snow for drinking, cooking, and cleaning. The daily chores fill up the hours, and night comes early this far north. I'm asleep by eight o'clock.

A knock at the door in the middle of winter is an unheard of event. When that unexpected noise reached my slumbering ears one January night, I blamed it on a dream and burrowed deeper into my sleeping bag. The sound came again, and I opened my eyes. The fire in the woodstove gave off a weak glow, reminding me that it needed another log or two. I unzipped the sleeping bag and squirmed free, slipping my stocking feet into untied boots. In the long underwear that never leaves my body between the months of October and June, I shuffled to the stove and tossed in two pieces of seasoned oak, closed the door, and turned the handle to the locked position.

Now wide-awake, I replayed the earlier noise. Unlike a branch scraping the side of the building, and unlike the clumsy clawing of a wild animal, this had been a rap, a melody, something with purpose behind it.

I grabbed my rifle and inserted the pre-loaded clip. I'm not a gun person, but out here…a woman alone… Well, you need a good weapon.

With the rifle in my hand, I opened the cabin door to the blue haze of a half moon falling on a world of white snow. Silence. So silent I could hear my own heart beating, and hear the blood running through my veins. But a new sound invaded. A mewling, like a newborn kitten. I looked down. Not far from my booted feet was a picnic basket.

Now I'm freaking out. Now my heart is slamming. In all the years I've lived here nothing has scared me. But I'm scared now.

I grabbed a flashlight and panned the area. Tracks. Sled-dog tracks leading off into the timber. A single set of footprints coming and going. Was I dreaming? Worse yet, had I truly lost my mind? This seemed a plausible explanation.

The basket repeated the earlier sound. That pitiful cry.

I put the gun aside and flipped open one half of the lid. Inside the basket, lying atop a blue blanket, was a note printed in Times New Roman font.

"Please care for this infant. His name is James. A representative will pick him up on October 31, 2016." I moved the flashlight beam along the paper, revealing a faint logo at the bottom. The entwined letters CC.

Clone Clone. Wow. Never expected to hear from them. I'd all but forgotten about the company responsible for paying for my bills. And after six or seven years and no special assignment, I'd started thinking of this place as mine. Now I resented their intrusion into my Utopia even though they were responsible for that Utopia.

This basket at my feet. Damn. A job. How unappealing. A baby. Even more unappealing. And what year was it now? 2011? Good grief. Could that be right? I rechecked the letter. Maybe it was a typo. How could I possible take care of a kid until 2016?

❖

The baby stayed five years. By age two he'd developed a swagger, and by age four it became obvious my ward was none other than James Dean. Five years and many months after the basket showed up on my porch, a bald man in a black trench coat arrived to take James away.

"In appreciation for your silence, loyalty, and excellent service, we are offering to clone someone for you free of charge," the CC representative said while little James pounded the man's wingtip shoe with a toy hammer. "Who would you like?"

My own clone. The equivalent of hush money. Their cloning operation would be at risk of being shut down if word ever got out that they were reproducing famous people.

"Johnny Depp? How about Johnny Depp?" the man asked. "Would you like to have your own Johnny Depp? Sean Connery?

How about Sean Connery? Kurt Cobain? Jesus? Would you like your own Jesus Christ? Although that DNA is questionable."

"How about me?" I asked.

He did a little recoil combined with a blink. "You aren't anybody."

"I want another me."

"That seems a waste of the cloning process. The whole idea behind Clone Clone is to reproduce celebrity. Reproduce someone who's had a cultural impact on society. And let me remind you that the package we're offering for free is normally a million dollars."

"I did raise James Dean," I pointed out. "He's potty trained. He knows how to dress himself. He can even write his own name. And I taught him to say: You're tearing me apart!"

"You're tearing me apart!" little James echoed, followed by a bounce, a double-handed whack of the hammer to the dress shoe, and a giggle.

"Quotes aren't a part of our manifesto, but we appreciate your hard work," the man said as he struggled unsuccessfully to keep the pain from his voice. "We appreciate your getting him through the unpleasant early years. Our buyers don't want infants. They really want fully mature products, but obviously that's impossible. Many clients don't understand that the clone has to grow just like any human."

"You said you'd clone anybody for me."

"I know, but we think along the lines of famous people. I mean, of course we have our boundaries. We wouldn't clone a Charles Manson or an Ed Gein. That would be unethical."

"How many times have you heard someone say 'I wish I could clone myself'?" I asked. "Well, I'm saying it right now."

He sighed, and his shoulders dropped in resignation. "The board won't like this."

He collected some of my DNA skin cells and then left with little James Dean. To tell the truth, I was sorry to see the child go, but glad to have the place to myself once more.

The following October, Halloween to be exact, a knock sounded on my cabin door. I opened it to find a picnic basket on the porch. From inside came a soft mewling. Enclosed was a note: *If at any time this product does not meet your expectations, please don't hesitate to contact CC at our 800 number. We are all about the customer. And, if at any point your clone becomes a drag, please dispose of properly and remember, don't be a litterbug.*

Plaything

Daniel Hatadi

Small, piercing screams echoed off the walls of the Kids Playhouse, a converted factory where children of all shapes and sizes ran around like headless chickens, unaware that the special Halloween price of twenty bucks allowed for only two hours of fun.

Rushing out of the glassed parent's section, Manny and Tim bumped shoulders. Tim held his arm and stifled a sound, which probably meant he had bruises again. At least that's what he always told Manny. Tim quickly recovered and they ran and jumped over the ankle-high barrier of the under-fives playpen. Manny let out a shriek because they were both eight and it was fun to go where they weren't supposed to.

Hollow plastic balls in primary colours oozed around their feet as they stomped on the padded floor. Manny dived into the multi-coloured sea of plastic, surfacing with a choice yellow ball that he bounced off the back of Tim's curly blond head.

Manny used his arms like paddles, bobbing as he followed his friend deeper into the playpen. Tim's blond curls disappeared through a gap in the balls. Manny took a deep breath and blocked his nose before diving under the surface, waving his arms in front of him like a swimmer. Moments later he bumped against the wall and his hands brushed something furry.

Recoiling, he jumped up for air, arriving exactly where he'd planned, his back to the corner. There was no sign of Tim.

He scanned the crowd of toddlers, moving around the play-pen on his knees so none of the parents would tell him to leave. He crawled until it hurt, but he couldn't find his friend. He must have sneaked back around somehow. Maybe he'd worked out the same swimming trick.

Either that or the sea of plastic balls had swallowed him up.

❖

Back at the two long tables mostly filled with grownups on their mobile phones, Manny pulled at his dad's elbow. "I can't find Tim."

Manny's dad was talking to Tim's, a stocky man named Dave who looked like a lumberjack. The men were arguing about lawn mowers or cars or something. Dave ignored Manny and it took a few more elbow pulls for the boy to get his dad's attention.

"Hold on, Dave. What's up little fella?" Manny's dad said.

"Can't find Tim. We were playing over there." With a fully extended arm, Manny pointed to the playpen.

"Did he go to the little men's room? You sure he's not around?"

Manny nodded with his whole body.

"They're playing games, Joe. Rack off, Manny," Dave said. "Go find Tim yourself."

It was weird for Manny to hear his dad's name spoken, espe-cially coming from Tim's dad, the so-and-so that kept putting bruises on Tim's arm. Manny thought only stepdads did that. He really didn't like Tim's dad. Joe didn't either. Manny could tell.

Manny pulled at his dad's elbow again, looked up into deep brown eyes set below bushy eyebrows, until his dad could see that Manny really did need help. Running his hand through his much larger mop of dark hair that was just like Manny's, Joe stood up and gently took his son's arm.

"Okay, let's see where Tim's hiding."

❖

By now, the under-fives had been locked in the jungle-theme room, screaming out an incoherent Happy Birthday song. The playpen was filled with nothing but the plastic balls and some kid's Thomas-the-Tank-Engine backpack. Manny stayed just outside the playpen, elbows on the low wall, watching his dad stomp through the balls.

"There, in the corner, that's where he was," Manny said, hoping his dad would pull Tim up like a prize from a skill-tester machine. But Joe just wandered around the playpen, eventually ending up at the corner and kneeling down to look closely. He came back to Manny, holding what might have been the same yellow ball Manny had thrown at Tim. It was covered in dark, furry mold. That must have been the stuff Manny had brushed against.

"We have to tell the owners about this," Joe said, holding the ball up to the light. "After we check the toilets for Tim and tell his dad what's happened."

"This was supposed to be fun," Manny said. "I don't like Halloween anymore."

"Don't worry, we'll find him." Joe tousled Manny's hair. "Why don't you go play with the other kids and I'll sort this out, huh?"

❖

Manny ran behind the theme rooms, past the jungle room filled with under-fives, past the empty lolly-land room and extra quick past the open doors of the toilets, just to make sure none of the parents popped out and told him he wasn't allowed to be there.

He came to a padded dance floor that had a flashing strobe light and a screen filled with a young dancing Michael Jackson. Two girls played tag in the corner, tapping each other and bouncing off the walls, giggling non-stop. One of the girls tapped Manny on the shoulder and ran screaming to the other girl. She must have thought he wanted to play because she kept peeking out from behind her friend. What he was really trying to do was get a good look at the corner when the strobe was bright because he could see a dark stain that looked the same as the one in the playpen.

The strobe light flashed. Another step, another flash…step, flash, bump. They were in the corner now, the taller girl in front, trying her best to keep Manny from getting her friend. He moved back and stood still with his arms folded. The girl giggled and lunged at him. In the darkness of the corner, with his own body casting a shadow, Manny saw flashes of arms and open mouths and swaying pigtails and tiny skirts.

One more flash, and the taller girl stopped and her eyes opened wide: her friend was no longer behind her. Her friend was no longer anywhere.

Looking like she'd eaten a lemon that was about to make her sick, the girl raced past Manny in flashes highlighted by the strobe.

Manny put his face close to the mold. It was bigger than the mark from the playpen, almost the size of his own shadow. He didn't jump back this time even though he felt his heart pound and his clothes start to feel too hot on his skin. There was something that told him he was supposed to be here, having fun, as if he were playing with a friend. He could imagine himself talking to Tim right now.

It's my turn to hide. I'll bet you a handful of lollies you can't find me.

Let me see the lollies first.

I don't have them now, but I'll get —

Manny. I need your help.

This wasn't right. Manny was just imagining talking to Tim, just playing. It wasn't Tim's voice in his head. He couldn't be talking to him, Tim wasn't here.

Need help.

The mold in the corner looked funny under the flashing

strobe, like it was moving. Tiny holes swam like tadpoles. With every flash of the strobe, the holes turned into shapes. A mouth, a pair of eyes. A hint of a nose. They flitted about the surface until they became faces. And then there were lots of faces and some of them Manny could even recognise.

The girl that had disappeared. Some other kid he'd seen earlier in the jumping castle.

And finally, Tim.

Help me Manny. It says it will let us go. Bring someone else. Someone big. It says we're too small.

The mold swirled into a larger shape, buckled and swayed like it wasn't strong enough to hold itself together. Manny had only one strobe flash to see what it was.

The shape of a man.

❖

Joe yelled at Manny when he made it back to the grown-up's table. Said he shouldn't have run away like that, there were more kids missing now. They had to *evacmatate* the place or something, and they had to get everyone outside.

"Now."

"But Dad, Tim's still in here. We have to help him."

"That's what the police are for, son." Joe grabbed Manny's arm, tight this time. Manny decided not to try escaping just yet.

The parents and kids having Halloween parties were all trying to fit through the warehouse door at the same time. So many people bumping up against each other like dodge-em cars. Manny carefully watched them as his dad dragged him to the door. And when a big burly man pushed himself between Joe and Manny, the boy broke free from his dad's grip. As he ran, he could hear the security guard tell his dad to stay put, but Manny kept running without looking back.

The padded dance room was well lit now and the screen was off. Manny headed straight for the corner, looking for the face in the mold, but it wasn't there. He searched the space, spotting something he hadn't seen when the strobe light was on: a passage in the other corner that went round, behind the padded wall.

Manny followed it and found a set of stairs that led up to the top of a huge yellow slippery slide. The small landing was covered in rugs that looked like sacks. They must be what people used to get down the slide nice and fast. Manny nodded to himself when he saw the three little runways that were just wide enough for a person. That's when Manny noticed that one of the sacks was covered in mold.

He picked it up, but when he saw the mold shift, he let the sack drop. The mold crept up the wall behind the top of the slide, and faces appeared just like before. This time the faces swarmed until one of them came clearly into view.

It was Tim's face.

"I tried to get them to come, but they wouldn't. I don't know what to do now, Tim. Everyone's leaving," Manny said.

The faces mutated into dozens of tiny hands, all spiralling together and around each other, eventually forming into a larger hand as big as Manny. The hand came forward, out of the wall, holding something. Then the mold fell, dropping what it held before swirling back to the wall and disappearing into the cracks. Manny looked at the floor.

Tim's shoe.

❖

Outside the play centre, parents and kids milled about like seagulls desperate for food. A police car had parked itself at an angle, blocking off entry to the lot. Which also meant no one was getting out. Manny scanned the area for Tim's dad. He would have to come once he saw Tim's shoe. Had to.

He found Joe and Dave together, leaning against Dave's black four-wheel-drive. The men were talking quietly, sneaking looks around the car park, especially towards the play-centre door.

Dave noticed Manny, but the boy couldn't tell what he was thinking. Couldn't tell if he was angry or scared or just didn't care.

Bring someone else. Someone big.

Manny held the shoe high for both men to see. "I found him. He caught his foot on the top of the slide. You have to come quick!" he said, all in one breath.

Dave smacked Manny in the back of the head. It came out of nowhere and hurt more because of the shock than actual pain. Manny put his hand where he was hit, and tried to stop himself from crying.

"You do that again and I'll knock you flat," Joe told Dave, giving him a look that Manny hadn't seen his dad make before. Like he was daring Dave to try again. "You hear me?"

Manny saw a whole bunch of looks cross Dave's face before he nodded.

"Well? Are we going in or what?" Joe said.

Dave glared at Manny like it was all Manny's fault and nodded once more without saying a word.

❖

They climbed the stairs. It was hard for Manny to keep up with the two men with their long legs and big boots, but they eventually made it to the top of the slide. It was quiet in the warehouse now. The background music had stopped. The endless happy screaming of kids was gone. Manny pointed, and Joe and Dave looked at the wall. A wall that had no marks on it.

"You said Tim was caught, Manny," Joe said. "Where is he?"

"I … he wasn't …" Manny stopped. They wouldn't have come if he'd told them the truth.

Dave pushed past Manny and Joe on the narrow landing. On the side furthest from the stairs was a rope ladder leading down to another play area.

"He's not here. There's no one here. Where'd you get that shoe you little…" Dave caught himself when Joe shifted his stance and gave another one of those looks.

Joe bent down next to Manny. "You've been playing all day, son. You better not be playing now. Is Tim here?"

Manny nodded a few times, holding back tears. Tim was gone, and there was nothing he could do. He looked at his dad, looked right in his eyes and felt terrible for messing this up. He swallowed and the room went still. The three of them were silent and the sounds of cars and people outside the play centre faded away.

Something moved behind Joe. One of the slide sacks flapped about like a breeze was blowing through it. Another sack moved and Manny could see a dark shadow shift through the material, gathering quickly. It pooled around Joe's feet and crept up his boots.

Manny dropped Tim's shoe and pointed at the sacks. As the shoe tumbled down the slide, everything slowed like the hands on a clock with a flat battery.

Joe stood, tried to brush the mold off with his hands, but every time he touched it the mold reached out to cover him even more. He flailed as Dave jumped down the slide, not even bothering with a sack. Manny couldn't move, his heart pumping out of his chest, his finger still pointing at Joe.

Mold covered his father's legs, shorts, t-shirt, racing now along his arms, up his neck. Joe jumped around, almost falling down the slide, trying to get away from the thing that was taking him over. Manny watched as it covered his father and grew into some kind of giant, smelling of damp and earth like the space underneath a house. And when the thing had grown large enough to reach the roof of the warehouse, faces swam through the surface of the mold. The faces grew and took on the colours of flesh and hair. Eyes that were black holes appeared, then hands and arms and feet.

And then it happened.

Spilling out like fish dropped from a net onto a boat's deck, children poured from the shambling giant of mold, all the children that had disappeared. A kid with a red beanie. Another one from the jumping castle. The girl from the dance room. A couple of them fell to the platform, and another hit the top of the slide and started down.

Tim landed at Manny's feet like a gift, coughing and spluttering, wiping his face and hair. Manny bent to help his friend, and the green and black giant with thick arms and legs and huge torso reached out a hand to Manny just the way his dad would. The boy began to cry. It should have been Dave caught by the fungus. It was supposed to be Dave.

The warehouse door opened. Police and people and light and noise came flooding in. The hand dissolved, the giant fell to the floor, and the mold swirled around the sacks and wall, slithering away to disappear through the cracks.

About the Authors

Patricia Abbott has published more than seventy-five stories in various literary and crime fiction venues. She won a Derringer Award in 2008 for "My Hero." Forthcoming stories will appear in *Crimespree Magazine, Needle, Crimefactory, Spinetingler* and other online publications. She lives in Detroit. She blogs at http://pattinase.blogspot.com/

Stephen Blackmoore is a writer of pulp, crime and horror fiction. He is the author of the novel *City of the Lost*, a dark urban fantasy coming out from DAW Books in 2012. His short stories and poetry have appeared in *Plots With Guns, Spinetingler, Thrilling Detective, Shots, Clean Sheets* and *Flashing in the Gutters*. He lives in Los Angeles and, just to buck the stereotype, is *not* working on a screenplay.

Spinetingler Award nominee **Paul D. Brazill** was born in Hartlepool, England, and lives in Bydgoszcz, Poland. His writing has appeared in print and electronic magazines such as *Dark Valentine Magazine, Crimefactory, Beat to a Pulp, A Twist of Noir* and *Needle—a Magazine of Noir*. His story "Guns of Brixton" is included in the 2011 Mammoth Book of Best British Crime and his blog is YOU WOULD SAY THAT WOULDN'T YOU? His irregular column, I DIDN'T SAY THAT, DID I? is at *Pulp Metal Magazine*.

Julia Buckley is a Chicago area writer. Her first mystery, *The Dark Backward* (2006), earned high praise from *Crimespree* and others. Her next book, *Madeline Mann*, received glowing reviews from *Kirkus* and *Library Journal*. Two Madeline Mann titles, *Madeline Mann* and *Lovely, Dark and Deep*, are available wherever ebooks are sold. Julia is a member of Sisters in Crime, MWA, and RWA. She keeps a writer's blog at *www.juliabuckley.blogspot.com* on which she interviews fellow mystery writers; her website is *www.juliabuckley.com*. She is currently at work on a new mystery series featuring an amateur sleuth and English teacher.

Bill Cameron is the author of the critically-acclaimed, Portland-based mysteries *County Line, Day One, Chasing Smoke,* and *Lost Dog*. His stories have appeared in *Killer Year, Portland Noir,* and the 2010 ITW anthology *First Thrills*. *Day One* was a Portland Mercury Best of 2010 selection. His books have been nominated for many awards, including the Spotted Owl for Best Northwest Mystery. Cameron lives in Portland, Oregon, where he is currently writing a young adult thriller.

The true face of **Heather Dearly** is one of wife, mother, and pleaser of real-name peoples. Troubled Water is her first published story. You can follow the nearest trail of twice-used tea bags to find her working on her next project, or you can follow her on Twitter. *http://twitter.com/heatherdearly* For more information, visit her blog at *http://heatherdearly.blogspot.com/*

Pat Dennis is the author of *Hotdish To Die For,* a collection of six culinary mystery short stories and 18 hotdish recipes. Her fiction and humor have been published in NPR's *Minnesota Monthly, Woman's World, The Pioneer Press, Sun Current Newspapers, Resort to Murder, The Silence of the Loons, Once Upon A Crime Anthology, Who Died In Here?, Hotdish Haiku,* and *Stand-Up and Die*. Pat is a stand-up comedian. Her 1,000 performances include comedy clubs, special events, Fortune 500 companies, women's expos and national television.

Jason Evans is a Philadelphia lawyer by day and a writer by night. He is the twilightkeeper at The Clarity of Night (http://clarityofnight.blogspot.com), a blog featuring fiction, poetry, photography, and sometimes cemeteries.

Paula L. Fleming is a very full-time freelance copy editor. When she gets time to write her own stories, she enjoys working in the genres of science fiction and fantasy, and she's slowly researching a fictionalized biography of children's author and illustrator Louise Fitzhugh. Paula lives in Minneapolis, Minnesota, with two large dogs, two cats, two tanks of fish, and one husband. She occasionally blogs about life and words at *http://paulafleming.home.comcast.net/*

Anne Frasier is a pseudonym of Theresa Weir (see page 192).

Daniel Hatadi has published several short stories and articles and is currently working on a novel. In 2007 he won the Spinetingler Magazine Special Services to the Industry Award for his work at CrimeSpace.ning.com. He has poems published in *The Lineup*, a chapbook of poetry from crime writers. His story, "Buddha Behind Bars," appears in the second Thuglit anthology, *Sex, Thugs and Rock & Roll.*

David Housewright is a reformed newspaper reporter and ad man who earned the 1996 Edgar Award for Best First Novel from the Mystery Writers of American. His second novel received a Shamus nomination from the Private Eyes Writers of America. *Practice to Deceive* won a 1998 Minnesota Book Award and *Jelly's Gold* earned the same prize in 2010. His tenth novel, The *Taking of Libbie, SD*, was published in June of 2011. Housewright's short stories have appeared in publications as diverse as *Ellery Queen's Mystery Magazine* and *True Romance* as well as anthologies *Silence of the Loons, Twin Cities Noir*, and *Resort to Murder.*

Mark Hull claims that he couldn't write his way out of a paper bag using an X-Acto knife for a pen, yet he perseveres. He lives the life of an anchorite in St. Paul, Minnesota, and has as pets two quolls and a numbat, the latter of which is not yet house-trained. When he's not praying or wrangling marsupials, he participates in a number of "social networking" applications on the Internet and wishes he had a real life. Mark once played a stalker in a movie, and is currently working on a screenplay that you will be seeing in a theater near you Any Day Now.

A writer since childhood, **Leandra Logan** was thrilled to sell her first young adult romance novel in 1986. Since that time she has written a great number of books for both teenage and adult audiences. Her books routinely make the B. Dalton and Waldenbooks lists. As well, she has been nominated for numerous awards within the industry.

Michael Allan Mallory is the co-author of *Killer Instinct* and *Death Roll*, both written with Marilyn Victor. *Death Roll* (2007) introduced mystery's first zoologist sleuth and revealed what goes on behind the exhibits of a major metropolitan zoo. *Killer Instinct* (2011) finds zookeeper Lavender "Snake" Jones in the North Woods of Minnesota investigating a wild wolf killing and a double murder. Michael's short stories have appeared in several mystery anthologies. He works in the Information Technology field and lives in St. Louis Park, Minnesota, with his delightful wife and an elderly Maine Coon cat. His website is www. snakejones.com

Kelly Lynn Parra's earliest stories were told with paintbrushes, but upon discovering the drama and danger of suspense novels, those paintbrushes were replaced with a keyboard. Now a multi-published author, she has created memorable characters such as a graffiti artist, a psychic teen, and a tough undercover narc. A two-time RITA finalist, she divides her time between her novels, freelance writing, and the adventures of mother-hood where the zombies only live in her head, while she juggles her home life with two children, a tattooed husband, a sweet poodle, and a stealth turtle. To learn more about Kelly and her writing visit www.kellyparra.com

L. K. Rigel lives in California with her cat, Coleridge. She wrote songs for the 90s band The Elements, scored the independent science fantasy karate movie *Lucid Dreams*, and was a reporter for the Sacramento *Rock 'N Roll News*. Her work has appeared in *Literary Mama* and *Tattoo Highway*. She is the author of the In Flagrante Apocalypto series.

When writing her bio for the popular Ophelia and Abby series from Avon Books, **Shirley Damsgaard** noticed that many authors started theirs with the words, "I wanted to be a writer all of my life and wrote my first story at the age of five." She honestly can't say that—at the age of five, as an only child growing up on a farm, her career goal was to be a princess. Unfortunately, all those positions happened to be filled, so she followed the path so many other women have traveled—marriage, children, a career outside of the home—in her case, with the United States Postal Service. It wasn't until the tender of age of 48 that she decided to try her hand at writing. Now seven years and seven books later, she still lives in the same small town that she has for over twenty years, still has a career as postmaster, and her grown children, with their children, all live within driving distance. She still enjoys gardening, reading, and needlepoint, but her world is larger thanks to Ophelia and Abby.

Marilyn Victor is half of the writing team of Marilyn Victor and Michael Allen Mallory, known for their zoo mysteries. An animal lover since she could walk, Marilyn was a volunteer at the Minnesota Zoo for many years and shares her home with a revolving menagerie of homeless pets she fosters for a local animal rescue organization. She loves reading and writing all book genres and besides co-authoring the Snake Jones mystery series, she has a short story in the *Once Upon A Crime* anthology and is working on a paranormal adventure story.

Theresa Weir is a *USA Today* bestselling author of nineteen novels that span the genres of suspense, mystery, thriller, romantic suspense, and paranormal. Her books have been translated into twenty languages. Weir's debut title was the cult phenomenon *Amazon Lily*, initially published by Pocket Books and later reissued by Bantam Books. She won a RITA for romantic suspense (*Cool Shade*), and a year later the Daphne du Maurier for paranormal romance *(Bad Karma)*. Writing as Anne Frasier, her thriller and suspense titles (including *Hush, Sleep Tight, Play Dead*) were featured in Mystery Guild, Literary Guild, and Book of the Month Club. *Hush* was both a RITA and Daphne du Maurier finalist. Her memoir, *The Orchard*, is scheduled for a 2011 release by Grand Central Publishing. She lives in St. Paul, Minnesota, and rural Wisconsin.

Lance Zarimba lives in a haunted house built by the man who invented Old Dutch potato chips. He works as an occupational therapist in Minneapolis, MN, helping people with hand and finger injuries. He grew up watching *Dark Shadows* in the Upper Peninsula of Michigan and enjoys all of the classic monster movies. His mystery, *Vacation Therapy*, along with two children's books—*Oh No, Our Best Friend is a Zombie*, and *Oh No, Our Best Friend is a Vampire*—are newly released. His short stories have appeared in *Mayhem in the Midlands*, Pat Dennis's *Who Died in Here? 25 mystery stories of crimes and bathrooms*, Jay Hartman's *The Killer Wore Cranberry* for Untreed Reads, and eshort stories on Echelon Press. He can be reached at LanceZarimba@yahoo.com